Morton Prince

**The Nature of Mind**

and human automatism - Vol. 1

Morton Prince

**The Nature of Mind**
*and human automatism - Vol. 1*

ISBN/EAN: 9783337370411

Printed in Europe, USA, Canada, Australia, Japan

Cover: Foto ©Andreas Hilbeck / pixelio.de

More available books at **www.hansebooks.com**

# THE NATURE OF MIND

### AND

## HUMAN AUTOMATISM.

′ BY

## MORTON PRINCE, M.D.,

PHYSICIAN FOR NERVOUS DISEASES, BOSTON DISPENSARY; PHYSICIAN FOR NERVOUS
DISEASES, OUT-PATIENT DEPARTMENT, BOSTON CITY HOSPITAL, ETC.

PHILADELPHIA:

· J. B. LIPPINCOTT COMPANY.

LONDON: 15 RUSSELL STREET, COVENT GARDEN

1885.

# PREFACE.

THE basis of the following work was written some eight or nine years ago during my student days at the medical school, and afterwards served as a graduation thesis. Having been urged to publish this thesis by my friends, it was enlarged between two and three years ago to its present size. I do not think that the views expressed in the earlier essay have been changed in any important particular, though the phraseology has been in many passages altered, partly to make it harmonize with the conventional forms of expression used generally by writers on this subject, and partly because mature reflection made me aware that some of the original terms and phrases employed either did not correctly explain my meaning, or were lacking in precision and consequently capable of different interpretations. Many points which were of necessity merely touched upon in the earlier essay and hence liable to misinterpretation, have been since greatly expanded, and, especially in the chapter on "Self-Determination," explained more fully, extended reasons being given for the conclusions expressed. The final chapter, on "Materialism," has been entirely added. As I have pursued my studies on this subject, the views of other writers have been so far incorporated and criticised as has been thought would make the subject-matter clearer.

iii

The primary object of this book is to discuss certain problems of mind and matter—particularly the relation between the mind and the brain—simply as questions of psychology and physiology, without regard to the bearing they may have on philosophical doctrines. Still, all such questions lie so deeply at the root of the latter, that it is impossible to discuss the one without regarding the effect they have upon the other. Hence I have not hesitated to enter into the doctrine of Materialism so far as it is affected by the conclusions arrived at. Such questions as the relation of the mind to the body constitute the foundation of Spiritualism and Materialism. The latter, as a result of the great advancement which has been made by science during the last half-century, has of recent years awakened renewed interest and discussion. This has been directly due in no small degree to the writings of such men, among others, as Spencer, Huxley, Clifford, and Maudsley, in England, Vogt, Moleschott, and Büchner, in Germany, who, whether all of them have espoused materialistic opinions or not, have at any rate given new energy to the materialistic school, and aroused the opposition of the anti-materialists. It is not always easy, however, to correctly classify many prominent writers, as so much that is directly contradictory is found in their writings. It is not uncommon to read on one page that a given author emphatically denies materialism, and on the next to find what is apparently the most pronounced materialism. But, notwithstanding the strong ground on which it is intrenched, and the great help which it has received from science, materialism has met with strong opposition. Its opponents, it must be confessed, have made their attacks from all sides, with considerable vigor, and effectively brought to bear arguments based on philosophy and science. And yet, in spite of all its short-comings, materialism is essentially the philosophy of science, and hence that which must eventually prevail. All attacks against it have served only to show its weak places, not to break it down. Still, it cannot be denied that some of the objections urged against such forms of materialism as have been maintained by even its ablest advocates have been well founded. This, it seems to me, has not been the fault of the doctrine, but rather of its expounders. Not only have false meanings been attributed to it by its opponents, but even its advocates have not always understood its first principles, and the conclusions which have been drawn from scientific data have sometimes been directly in contradiction to the teachings of experience. Whatever merit the views advocated in the following pages may have, it is to be hoped that they at least harmonize some of the hitherto conflicting theories and facts, and that the really valid objections to materialism are avoided. In the maintenance of the materialistic nature of mind, certain difficulties have almost universally been recognized, especially on the side of " automatism," " self-determination," and in the application of the law of the Correlation of Forces, etc., which it has been difficult to overcome. Nay, more, while it has been seen that mind is to be regarded as some sort of " manifestation of matter," yet most writers are ready to admit the impossibility of explaining the exact connection between the two, and confess an insoluble mystery. Many of the most thoroughgoing materialists content themselves with stating the intimate union of the mental and physical worlds, without attempting to explain *how* they are united. The views maintained in the following pages, it is thought, both overcome these difficulties and furnish a satisfactory explanation of many of the mysteries of the mind, including its relation to the body and other kindred questions. The conclusions expressed as to the nature of the mind avoid, I believe, the objections which have proved fatal to other materialistic doctrines.

There is one writer whose writings I regret to have overlooked until long after this work was completed, and a short time before going to press. I refer to the late Professor Clifford, who, so far as I know, is the only writer whose views on the relation of the mind to the body coincide with those expressed in these pages. I regret that it was not practicable to refer to Clifford's writings more fully in the text, but references have been made in foot-notes when there appeared to be reason for doing so.

The original essay was withheld from print during these many years for several reasons, not the least among them being the desire to reflect well on so difficult a subject, which has already baffled some of the ablest minds the world has ever produced, before committing myself to a public expression of opinion. But I may add that continued study and maturer thought has only strengthened me in the views originally formed.

Boston, March, 1885.

# CONTENTS.

# PART II.

## HUMAN AUTOMATISM.

---

### CHAPTER I.

#### THE REFLEX CHARACTER OF IDEAS.

### CHAPTER II.

#### CONSCIOUSNESS AS AN AGENT IN THE DETERMINATION OF BODILY ACTION.

### CHAPTER III.

#### SELF-DETERMINATION.

# CHAPTER IV.

### WHAT IS MATERIALISM?

# PART I.

# THE NATURE OF MIND.

"THE very idea of so noble, so refined, so immaterial, and so exalted a being as the anima, or even the animus, taking up her residence, and sitting dabbling, like a tadpole, all day long, both summer and winter, in a puddle, or in a liquid of any kind, how thick or thin soever, he would say, shocked his imagination: he would scarce give the doctrine a hearing."—*Tristram Shandy*, B. ii. ch. 19.

# CHAPTER I.

## THE MODERN DOCTRINE OF THE RELATION OF THE MIND TO THE BODY.

" WHEN men have once acquiesced in untrue opinions," remarks Hobbes, " and registered them as authenticated records in their minds, it is no less impossible to speak intelligibly to such persons than to write legibly on a piece of paper already scribbled over." Hence it is that any inquiry like that which is the subject of this work is fraught with difficulties, which are due as much to the fact that most men have already acquiesced, without question, in opinions of transmitted authority as to the inherent obscurity of the matter. And although those, who have given especial thought to such questions, and from the stand-point of modern science have studied anew the problem of the relationship of the mind to the body, have arrived at conclusions differing largely from the orthodox beliefs held by the majority of even educated people, still, for a long time to come, it cannot be expected that these conclusions will be very widely accepted, until at least radical changes are made in modern methods of education. And yet, if all men could and would wipe out from their minds, as with a sponge, all existing opinions on such matters, and would begin anew to build up a doctrine of the nature of mind which should be in harmony with existing knowledge, there can be no doubt that a very different opinion would be arrived

at than that which obtains to-day. It is very difficult
for any one, brought up with certain ideas and beliefs,
to sufficiently set aside these preconceived notions to
give due weight to evidence offered by those of an opposed way of thinking. This is one of the reasons,
aside at least from the inherent difficulty of the subject
and the lack of exact knowledge of the mechanism of
the nervous system, why there has been so much difference of opinion regarding the relation of the mind to
the body, and why the opinion maintained by the gen-
erality of people differs so widely from that held by the
leaders in advanced thought. But though there is a
wide chasm between the notions of the unlearned and
the scientific writers of the day, there is an equally
wide one between the latter and another class of men,
who, though learned in such matters, still, from the
force of conservatism, adhere to ancient scholastic
creeds. The philosophical world to-day is divided, as
it always has been, into two schools of philosophy,—
the spiritual and the material, though the latter may
be said to be the exponent of modern science.

Spiritualism endeavors to explain all mental phenomena by presupposing the existence of a spiritual
something acting through the brain as its instrument:
materialism looks to the properties of matter alone for
a solution. But while spiritualism simplifies the problem by postulating what in one sense may be considered a definite, if incomprehensible, factor, materialism
on the other hand, protean in its forms, embraces many
doctrines and appears under many guises. Spiritualism simply avoids the difficulty by going around it;
materialism boldly enters the labyrinth, but often

becomes lost in its mazes. Materialism, like spiritualism, was originally the creation of metaphysical
speculation, and contained very little that was founded
upon established fact. As long as this was the case,
as long as materialism was but the product of abstract
speculation without positive scientific data upon which
to rest, it was nothing more than a mere collection of
fanciful hypotheses, without solidity and without sub-
stantial support. In this respect it was like unto its
opponent spiritualism, and only merited the neglect
it formerly received. It is only within the last few
decades that sufficient evidence has been collected, as
the result of patient and laborious investigation into
the phenomena of nature, to justify the offering of
materialism as a satisfactory explanation of the phe ·
nomena of the universe and to warrant its acceptance.
With every addition to our knowledge, with every fresh
discovery in the domains of science, the deeper we pene-
trate into the mysteries of nature, the stronger becomes
the doctrine of modern materialism; until to-day it
offers the most acceptable explanation of the vital
problems with which science has to deal. It is difficult
to understand how any one, who has taken pains to
thoroughly inform himself on the great scientific questions of the day and is conversant with the discoveries
made of late years in the natural sciences, especially in
the department of biology, can fail to find in materialism[1] the most satisfactory explanation that has yet been

---

[1] It is only fair to say that by materialism I do not mean any
of those crude notions which are commonly attached to the term.
By materialism I mean a much higher form of doctrine, which
I believe to be the legitimate expression of the scientific thought

offered of vital phenomena. It is true that what has been accomplished is insignificant compared with what remains to be done, but with every step forward the way becomes clearer and the path surer. In these pages we shall be interested only with that aspect of materialism which deals with the relation between mind and body ; an old question, but one which so far from becoming hackneyed with time, receives increasing interest from every additional discovery made in the physiology of the nervous system. We are to-day, for the first time, just beginning to be in a position to investigate the problem which nervous physiology alone has properly opened to us and which before has remained as a sealed book. All metaphysical speculation, not founded on physiological data, as to its contents must be looked upon as a series of more or less shrewd guesses, and even with our present knowledge of the functions of the nervous system, we cannot consider that we have more than arrived at the threshold of the inquiry. The time has not yet arrived when we can hope to thoroughly understand the relations of the mental to the physical world. Nevertheless, as the merchant from time to time stops in the midst of his transactions to "take account of stock," so in the progress of science, it is well to occasionally pause, and cast

---

of the day, though perhaps it is necessary to admit that some of the exponents of this thought reject, for what appears to me insufficient reasons, the term materialism. This may be because this expression has often been invested with a meaning, crude and unphilosophical, with which this higher form has nothing in common. What is understood by materialism will be explained in the final chapter, to which the reader is referred.

our eyes over what has been done, to sum up the evidence that has been accumulated, and see whither we are drifting. Accordingly, the writer has ventured in these pages to call attention to that explanation of the problem which seems most in accordance with the present condition of science. The subject has been approached entirely from a materialistic stand-point, and therefore the spiritualist will probably find little herein to disconcert him. In a subject so prolific in literature as that of the relation of mind and matter, no one can hope to invent a theory that has not at some time or other been previously suggested. At most one can only hope, as fresh additions are made to our knowledge, to bring new and more potent evidence in support of this or that theory, and to read more intelligently by the light of improved science problems that before have been involved in obscurity and veiled in mysticism. In the following pages the writer has simply endeavored to bring forward evidence in support of a theory which has seemed to him most in accordance with known facts, and to explain by natural means phenomena which otherwise border on the mysterious. The doctrines which are maintained have seemed to him to be the only logical sequences of the generally accepted views held to-day in regard to the basis of mental processes, and if the latter are accepted the other should be also. How far the views here advocated are in harmony with those of other writers will be noticed later.

If we look a little more closely into the history of philosophy, it will be found that it has always been a tendency of mankind to explain the unknown by a

resort to mysterious and supernatural agents. This
has been true both of animate and inanimate nature.
It is a tendency which has prevailed in inverse proportion to the existing knowledge of the causation of
natural phenomena. The wind, the thunder, the lightning, the properties of matter, all have at different
times been explained by means of supernatural or immaterial agents. Mind has been no exception to this
law; but as the cloud which has hung over our knowledge of biological processes has remained longer un-
lifted than in other departments of science, the spiritual
influence has been longer felt, and mental phenomena
have remained for a longer time enshrouded in
mysticism.

To-day the weight of authority is in favor of a
material basis for all mental phenomena. It is generally conceded that mind depends upon the development of a peculiar matter, the brain, for its existence.

The brain is a complex organ made up of what are
called nerve-cells and nerve-fibres, the latter serving as
conductors, like ordinary telegraph-wires, for the cells,
which are the batteries which run the nervous mechanism. Of the nerve-fibres, some connect together the
neighboring cells, others cells situated in distant parts
of the brain. Other systems of fibres connect the
brain with the various parts of the body. Of these
latter there are two kinds: one ingoing, called the
sensory or centripetal nerves, which convey impressions to the cells of the brain; and the other, outgoing, called motor, or centrifugal, which convey excitations from the cells of the brain to the muscles,
viscera, and other parts. This, in a rough way, is

the anatomical mechanism of the nervous system.
The more minute structure with still other systems
of nerves it is not necessary for our purpose to consider. We have here what is called a nervous loop.
An impression is conveyed from the skin, for example, by way of the ingoing nerves to the brain.
Here an agitation[1] is set up among the molecules
of the cells. -This agitation is conveyed from cell
to cell, a greater or less number being implicated as
the case may be; and finally this molecular motion
is retransmitted as a nervous current along the outgoing nerves to the muscles to end in muscular action.
Now the important point is this: at the moment
when the ingoing current reaches the cerebral molecules, a feeling of some sort arises in the individual,
and continues as long as these molecules continue in
agitation, and ceases when the molecular motion ceases.
Whenever the molecules of the brain are set into activity, a sensation or thought of some kind occurs;
and, *vice versa*, whenever a thought or sensation arises,
a corresponding molecular agitation occurs. Let us
take a concrete example. A man is sitting in his
library quietly reading. The rays of light from his
book fall upon his retina and excite the terminal fila-
ments of the optic nerve; from here the impression is
carried as a neural current to the brain, and excites the
molecules of the cells. Along with this excitement of
the cerebral molecules there arises the image called the
book, and all the various thoughts corresponding to the
printed words of the page. These thoughts are said

---

[1] Often called undulations, tremors, vibrations, etc.

to occur side by side with the molecular agitation. Suddenly the cry of " fire" is raised. The man throws down his book, jumps from his chair, and runs down stairs in answer to the alarm. Now what has occurred in his nervous apparatus? The pulsations of the atmosphere corresponding to the sound " fire" have struck upon his auditory apparatus; from there they have been conveyed as a neural undulation or current along the auditory nerve to his brain and there aroused a new set of molecular motions; and with them a new set of thoughts has arisen, embracing perhaps a mental picture of the house in flames and of danger to the inmates. But not stopping here, the cerebral motion has been transmitted along the outgoing nerves to the muscles, and resulted in the actions just described; we have here, from a physical point of view, what is called a nervous circuit. On the one hand we have a series of molecular motions beginning with irritations of sensory nerves, and passing as cerebral motions through the brain, ending in muscular action; and on the other hand we have states of consciousness correlated with a portion of that circuit, the cerebral portion. In this or in some modified form of this consists all nervous and mental action. On this fact is based the doctrine of the physical basis of mind, which recognizes the association and interdependence of molecular motions and consciousness. Underneath, then, every mental act there flows a physical current. With every thought, sensation, or emotion is associated a physical change in a material substance,—the brain. No mental act can take place without a corresponding physical change; no physical change without a corresponding mental act. Such is the usually accepted doctrine of the present day.

According to this view we have two sets of phenomena, two classes of facts, a mental act and a physical change, invariably associated together. But this is very far from explaining the nature of mental processes. The further question is here presented to us, What is the nature of this association? Is it to be looked upon, as many think, as a mere *coexistence* of dissimilar phenomena, rather than as one in which any dependency of the one upon the other can be traced? And are we here to place a limit to our inquiries, and consider that the problem has been reduced to its lowest terms? If we are content to do so, very little progress can be said to have been made towards understanding the relationship between mind and matter. Unless some causal or interdependent relation between the two can be established, we shall be very little better off than we were before physiological science undertook to solve the problem.

But, in truth, physiological science does pretend to go further, though a careful study of the teachings of the exponents of the modern school will reveal two different interpretations of the facts, however unanimous they may appear at first sight. These two interpretations may be termed the Theory of Functions and the Theory of Aspects. Both theories I hope to be able to show are neither a sufficient nor correct explanation of the facts.

The basis of both doctrines is a physical substance underlying both series of facts,—the physical disturbances, and consciousness,—but the relation which the two series bear to this substance differs in the two theories.   First, as to the Theory of Functions.

After a careful study of the reasoning by which this conclusion has been reached, as well as of the general meaning which seems to underlie the writings of the principal authorities on the subject, I am convinced that there is only one intelligible meaning with which this doctrine can be invested, and that is this: there is one underlying matter or substance; this substance has two properties,—one of these properties is known as those disturbances we call nerve-motions, the other is consciousness; that is, our ideas, sensations, and emotions.   When nerve-motions, the one "property" of this matter, is present, consciousness, the other "property," appears simultaneously.   Both come and both go side by side together; but *why* when one appears the other should do so also we do not know.   They may be likened to the following ideal case.   Let us invest a piece of iron with the properties of magnetism and heat under ideal conditions.   Let us suppose (which is not the case) that whenever the temperature of the iron is raised above that of the surrounding air it becomes magnetized, and, conversely, whenever it becomes magnetized the temperature becomes raised. In this case the magnetism could be said to correspond with consciousness and heat with nerve-motions.

This simile must not be pushed farther than is intended.   In this case of the iron the heat will probably be inferred to be the cause of the magnetism, and *vice versa.*   But this has scarcely been asserted to be the case with mind and the accompanying neural undulations.   The analogy is applicable only so far as con-

cerns the parallelism of the phenomena. Consciousness and nerve-motions are said only to run in parallel
circuits. When one is present, the other is also present. They resemble two clocks, which, wound up at
the same moment, record the time and strike the hours
in perfect harmony. "We can trace," says Tyndall,
"the development of a nervous system, and correlate
with it the *parallel phenomena of sensation and thought.*
We see with undoubting certainty that they go hand
in hand. But we try to soar in a vacuum the moment
we seek to *comprehend the connection between them;*" [1]
and yet "thought," says Huxley, "is as much a function
of matter as motion is." [2]

Although the theory has not often, if at all, been
stated as distinctly or boldly as has just been done, still
I think I am justified in this interpretation of it. This
is the general idea underlying this form of the materialistic doctrine, and is the only meaning which can
be deduced from the writings of such men as have accepted it, although it may be suspected that the very
vagueness with which it is often stated is not indicative
of a clear conception of the defined conditions. Furthermore, this interpretation is the only one which is
*logically compatible with the deductions which have been
drawn from the doctrine itself.* This I hope to be able
to show later. Till then I shall have to ask the reader
to provisionally accept it. According to this doctrine
we may be said to have to do with a unity of substance and a duality of properties.

The Theory of Aspects differs considerably from this,

---

[1] Belfast Address, p. 62.  [2] On Descartes.

though the two are sometimes confused and regarded as identical.   There is certainly often lacking that precision of language which is essential to a clear understanding of the problem.

According to the Theory of Aspects, consciousness and nerve motions (vibrations) are only different aspects of one and the same underlying substance, which is unknown.   This view has perhaps been as clearly expressed by Bain, as by any one else, when he says, " the one substance with two sets of properties, two sides (the physical and the mental), a double-faced unity, would seem to comply with all the exigencies of the case." [1]

The same notion has thus been described by Lewes : "There may be every ground for concluding that a logical process has its correlative physical process, and that the two processes are merely two aspects of one event." [2]   And again : " The two processes are equivalent, and the difference arises from the difference in the mode of apprehension." [3]

The inadequacy of these theories of Functions and Aspects to explain much of the difficulty is admitted by most writers almost in the same breath in which they advanced them.   That which has received the most general acceptance is the Theory of Aspects, but as an explanation it is incomplete.   To say that consciousness is the subjective aspect of matter is equivalent to saying that consciousness is the conscious side of matter, which is no explanation.   It is simply stating over again in different terms the fact we wish

---

[1] Mind and Body, p. 196.
[2] Physical Basis of Mind, p. 395.                    [3] Ibid.

to explain; and similarly, to say that nerve-motion is the objective aspect of the same matter is simply to say that nerve-motions are objective phenomena, which is what we knew before. These are only restatements of the facts, not explanations of them. Nor does it help matters to say that the same matter underlies both, or the difference between them is due to different modes of apprehending the same thing. I shall have more to say on this point in chapter iv., to which the reader is referred. What we wish to know is this: *How do we come to have two aspects instead of one ?* Why, when we have one aspect, should we also have at the same time the other? How is the one set of changes, the physical, related to the other set, the mental? What is that connection between them that insures the presence of a feeling when physical disturbances are produced, or when a feeling is present, induces physical disturbances? *What difference is there between the essential nature of an objective fact, like a neural tremor, and a subjective state or feeling, and have they anything in common ?* These are important questions which call for answers, and any doctrine which fails to explain them falls far short of the requirements of the case. But these questions, there need be no hesitation in saying, neither the theory of functions nor aspects explains. On the contrary, the former has led to deductions which, though logically drawn from the premises, are inconsistent with the facts established by each one's own consciousness. Consequently the premises must be false. The deductions I refer to I propose to consider in a later chapter, and therefore that discussion will not be anticipated here, further than to say that, accepting this explanation, it has been held by some, that states of consciousness are merely by-products, and in nowise essential to the working of the body; or, in other words, that our feelings have no causative influence in the production of our actions.  So that when I eat because (as I suppose) I am hungry, or work out an intricate mathematical problem, or strike some one who made me angry, I am not prompted to these acts, and do not carry them into execution under the direction of my thoughts and feelings, but these acts are done by the mechanism of the brain, and the chemical and physical changes which work the mechanism are simply *accompanied* by my feelings and thoughts, but not influenced in any way by them.  Our feelings become simply indicators, like those of a steam-engine, which tell the number of revolutions, and height of pressure, without in any way affecting the revolutions themselves.

Such a conclusion is sufficient to reduce the whole theory to an absurdity.

The inadequacy of the above explanations, however simple and satisfactory they may appear at first sight, is recognized on all sides, and is the same whether it be approached on the physical or on the subjective side. They simply avoid the difficulty, they do not remove it. This difficulty is, as I have said, in explaining *how we come to have two aspects,* and how these two "aspects" are related; how physical changes become translated into the subjective feeling.  That the two are correlated in time, that is, that the two occur simultaneously, side by side, is plain enough and easily understood, but it is confessedly not so easy to understand how the one becomes "transformed" (?) into the other; how, in fact, a feeling insures the presence of a physical motion, and a physical motion, of a feeling. Thus Mr. Spencer, who, as a psychologist, has treated the matter in a masterly manner, maintains this view of different aspects. "For what," he says, "is objectively a change in a superior nerve-centre is subjectively a feeling, and the duration under the one aspect measures the duration of it under the other."[1]  And the same thing is repeated in other passages.  But this is no explanation, as Mr. Spencer himself tacitly recognizes when he later adds, "though accumulated observations and experiments have led us by a very indirect series of inferences to the belief that mind and nervous action are the subjective and objective faces of the same thing, *we remain utterly incapable of seeing and even of imagining how the two are related.*  Mind still continues to us a something without any kinship to other things; and from the science which discovers by introspection the laws of this something, there is no passage by transitional steps to the sciences which discover the laws of these other things."[2]  Here is a mystery which he recognizes in common even with his spiritualistic opponents.

Professor Tyndall, as a physicist and avowed materialist, as one who finds in the properties of matter alone sufficient to account for everything in the universe, both for the objective phenomena about us, and for the subjective world of consciousness within, " bows

---

[1] Principles of Psychology, 2d ed., ii. p. 107.
[2] Ibid., p. 140.  The italics not in original.

his head in the dust before that mystery of the mind, which has hitherto defied its own penetrative power, and which may ultimately resolve itself into a demonstrable impossibility of self-penetration." [1]  While Professor Tyndall finds in matter alone sufficient to account for the existence of mind, he still recognizes the difficulty whereof we speak.  "The passage," he says, " from the physics of the brain to the corresponding facts of consciousness is unthinkable.  Granted that a definite thought, and a definite molecular action of the brain, occur simultaneously : we do not possess the intellectual organ, nor apparently any rudiment of the organs which would enable us to pass, by a process of reasoning, from one to the other.  They appear together, but we do not know why.  Were our minds and senses so expanded, strengthened, and illuminated as to enable us to see and feel the very molecules of the brain ; were we capable of following all their motions, all their groupings, all their electric discharges, if such there be ; and were we intimately acquainted with the corresponding states of thought and feeling, we should be as far as ever from the solution of the problem : How are these physical processes connected with the facts of consciousness?  The chasm between the two classes of phenomena would still remain intellectually impassable." [2]  " We may think over the subject again and again ; it eludes all intellectual presentation ; we stand at length face to face with the incomprehensible." [3]

It may be seen how insufficient is the boasted modern

[1] Apology for the Belfast Address.
[2] Scientific Materialism in Fragments of Science, p. 420.
[3] Apology for the Belfast Address.  Same, p. 560.

scientific doctrine as explained by Spencer and others, even to those who maintain it, by turning to the works of Mr. Fiske, a disciple and enthusiastic admirer of Mr. Spencer. " Henceforth," he says, " we may regard materialism as ruled out, and relegated to that limbo of crudities to which we some time since consigned the hypothesis of special creations. The latest results of scientific inquiry, whether in the region of objective psychology or in that of molecular physics, leave the gulf between mind and matter quite as wide as it was judged to be in the time of Descartes. It still remains as true as then, that between that of which the differential attribute is thought and that of which the differential attribute is extension, there can be nothing like identity or similarity. Although we have come to see that between the manifestations of the two there is such an unfailing parallelism that the one group of phenomena can be correctly described by formulas originally invented for describing the other group, yet all that has been established is this parallelism." [1]

Many other writers, physiologists and psychologists alike, might be quoted to the same effect, but it is hardly necessary.

It is naturally with considerable hesitation that one attempts to explain that which such thoughtful minds declare to be inexplicable, and yet it may fairly be questioned whether, after all, this " mystery" is not a dust of their own raising. It may be asked whether each, the physiologist and psychologist, has not approached the subject too much from his own point of

---

[1] Cosmic Philosophy, vol. ii. p. 445.

view to the exclusion of that of the other; whether
the physiologist has not paid too strict attention to the
physical phenomena to the neglect of facts of consciousness, while the psychologist has kept too steadily
in mind the data of consciousness and left out of sight
the physical side.   I would not be understood to insinu-
uate that either took no account of one or the other
side.   This would be merely presumptuous misstate-
ment.   On the contrary, both recognize one material
basis for both classes of facts; both recognize that the
presence of consciousness cannot be disassociated from
the physical changes which are supposed to accompany
it, and that we cannot have one without the other.
But after recognizing this, and indeed emphasizing it
and insisting upon it, they straightway take leave of
one another, and travel in different directions.

When discussing such a subtle subject as the nature
of the relation between mind and matter, it is necessary
to keep constantly before one both the facts which terms
represent and the ultimate analysis of those facts, and
to bear the whole of this ultimate analysis constantly
in mind.   For example, when we speak of a material
object we must constantly keep before us what we
really mean by this object; we must have before us the
notion of a number of sensations or states of our own
mind, such as extension, color, hardness, etc., which are
commonly, though of course erroneously, located in the
object itself; then the notion of the supposed something existing outside of us, and which is the cause of
those sensations; and, lastly, the inferred reaction between the two, by which the latter excite in us the
sensations we call properties of the object.   Unless the

whole of this is constantly remembered we are liable to be drawn into fallacies, for it is only in this way that in any given set of phenomena that which is subjective can be picked out and separated from that which is objective. In the simplest example of the objective world, as of a table or book, that which is subjective, and the creation of the mind is so interwoven with that which is objective, and which really exists outside of us, that only those learned in such matters can distinguish between them. Nine persons out of ten, if told that those physical characteristics which distinguish one picture from another—the beauty of the coloring, the grace of the drawing, and the "tone"—do not really belong to it, but exist as such only in the mind of the observer, would indignantly repel your insinuations, and if you still insisted upon it as a philosophical truth, you would be set down as a "crank" for your superior knowledge. Even the most acute thinkers, those most conversant with these truths, will sometimes fall into the pitfall of objectivity. Alexander Bain, for example, in chapter vi. on the Union of Mind and Body, remarks,—

"Walking in the country in spring, our mind is occupied with the foliage, the bloom, and the grassy meads,—all purely objective things; we are suddenly and strongly arrested by the odor of the May blossom; we give way for a moment to the sensation of sweetness: for that moment the *objective regards cease;* we think of nothing extended; we are in a state where extension has no footing; there is to us place no longer." [1]

---

[1] Loc. cit., p. 135. Italics not in original.

Now why is the sense of smell any less objective than the sense of sight? When we smell anything, how does the subjective element enter into it any more than it does in our mental condition when we see anything?· The odor called sweetness is as much objective as those sensations of sight which he calls "the foliage, the bloom, and the grassy meads." Sweetness is not extended to be sure, but that is simply because smell is not sight or touch. Sweetness is a sensation which we commonly ascribe to objects, such as a rose or an orange, and we say that it belongs to them as a property, and hence is objective.[1] Further, though sweetness is not extended, that which causes the sensation of sweetness is capable of being presented to us through the sense of vision, ideally or actually, and then becomes extended.

Perhaps the principal reason for the great hostility which the materialistic doctrine has evoked on all sides is to be found, as has been hinted above, in the deductions which some writers have seen fit to draw from it. Because mind is only a "manifestation of matter" it has been maintained in some quarters that consciousness plays an unessential part in our cerebral processes,

---

[1] It may be urged in objection that the pleasurable emotion accompanying the odor, being entirely a subjective state, eliminates the objective element from the whole. But this would be equally true of the sensations of sight, such as "the foliage, the bloom," etc. There is more of a subjective element about sight than smell, for a visual perception of an object is a compound sensation, made up of color, absence or presence of light, size and shape (extension), and the combining of these into an idea of the object is a process of judgment,—an entirely subjective state.

and has nothing to do with determining our actions. No less an authority than Professor Huxley has expressed the opinion that the "consciousness of brutes [and men] would appear to be related to the mechanism of the body simply as a collateral product of its working, and to be as completely without the power of modifying that working as the steam-whistle, which accompanies the work of a locomotive-engine, is without influence upon its machinery." The lecture in which he gave expression to this view exposed him, in consequence, to a storm of vituperation and abuse, which might have overwhelmed a less fearless and able man than Professor Huxley. That this conclusion should not be accepted is proper, because it is not in accordance with the facts, and therefore either the premises or the reasoning by which it was reached must be false. In this case I conceive it to be the premises. I shall refer to this point in a later chapter and in another connection. But, on the other hand, it must be admitted that these views are the logical deductions of that doctrine which represents matter and mind to be double but parallel properties of matter. In this context it will be interesting to notice how the same idea of double properties impregnates the thought of another vigorous thinker, Mr. Tyndall. He recognizes two difficulties, two alternatives, neither of which can he accept. He consequently "bows his head" in his acknowledged ignorance before "two incomprehensibles." The error is the same; it lies partly in his premises, and partly in not keeping in mind what is subjective and what is objective in the notion of motion. He says,—

"The discussion above referred to turns on the question, Do states of consciousness enter as links into the chain of antecedence and sequence, which give rise to bodily action and to other states of consciousness, or are they merely *by-products*, which are not essential to the physical processes going on in the brain? Speaking for myself, it is certain that I have no power of imagining states of consciousness interposed *between* the molecules of the brain, and influencing the transference of motion among the molecules. The thought 'eludes all mental presentation,' and hence the logic seems of iron strength, which claims for the brain an automatic action uninfluenced by states of consciousness. But it is, I believe, admitted by those who hold the automatic theory that states of consciousness are produced by the marshalling of the molecules of the brain; and this production of consciousness by molecular motion is to me quite as unthinkable as the production of molecular motion by consciousness. If, therefore, unthinkability be the proper test, I must equally reject both classes of phenomena. I, however, reject neither, and thus stand in the presence of two incomprehensibles instead of one incomprehensible."[1]

The difficulty lies here: if physical changes and consciousness are double and parallel properties, then, as the former is known to enter as a link in the dynamic circuit, the latter cannot, and must, therefore, be a *by-product*, without influence over our bodily actions. On the other hand, the conscious property cannot be

---

[1] Apology for the Belfast Address.

thought of as entering into the dynamic circuit, because of the error above insisted upon of confusing the
subjective side of the notion of molecules with the *real*
objective or unknown side, the molecules-in-them-
selves. This fallacy pervades the whole passage.

Even Bain has this idea of a double property.
" The only tenable supposition is that mental and
physical proceed together as undivided terms." (This
is not an explanation ; it is only a restatement of the
association of mental and physical states.) " When,
therefore, we speak of a mental cause, a mental agency,
we have always a *two-sided cause;* the effect produced is
not the effect of mind alone, but of mind in company
with body. That mind should have operated on the
body is as much as to say that a two-sided phenomenon, one side being bodily, can influence the body; it
is, after all, body acting upon body. *When a shock of
fear paralyzes digestion, it is not the emotion of fear in
the abstract or as a pure mental existence that does the
harm; it is the emotion in company with a peculiarly excited condition of the nervous system; and it is this condition of the brain which deranges the stomach."* [1]

Now, on the contrary, we are entitled to believe that
our mind does not deceive us in this respect, and that
it is the sensation of fear which deranges the stomach.
*How* it does it is another question, but *that* it does it is
beyond dispute. When, at the thought of something
disagreeable, we feel nausea and the stomach " rebels,"
I believe we are entitled to maintain that the disagreeable thought is the cause both of the nausea and the

---

[1] Mind and Body, p. 181. Italics not in original.

spasm of the stomach. When, at the thought of a delicious morsel, our "mouth waters," it is the thought itself, *par excellence,* which causes the flow of saliva. But *how* is the problem requiring solution. I do not think any one can read Mr. Bain's work without believing that his treatment of this part of the subject is vague and unsatisfactory.

One thing must be admitted as a logical consequence of this doctrine. If consciousness and neural processes are only collateral parallel phenomena, the former must be excluded from all part in that working of the body in which the latter enter as links in the circuit of neural undulations.

The difficulty is we have been looking too much through prismatic spectacles, and have seen one line as two.

Sufficient has been said to show not only how inadequate is the commonly accepted modern doctrine to explain the relation between mind and matter, but that this very doctrine, when carried to its logical consequences, leads to the denial of the truth of that conviction possessed by each one of us, that our feelings have something to do with the production of our actions. They become merely collateral products of the workings of the body.

But there is one writer to whom I wish to call attention, who for clearness of thought, precision of expression, and for correct use of terms has rarely been equalled by any writer on this subject. I refer to the late George H. Lewes, whose work on the Physical Basis of Mind has not received, at least in this country, the attention it merits. I know of no one who has so correctly appreciated the nature of the problem to be solved. To Mr. Lewes belongs the credit of being the first to offer an explanation of many of the difficulties of the problem; an explanation which in some respects must be accepted as final. And yet his conclusions I cannot accept, believing them not to be the logical outcome of his arguments. He maintains the view of difference in "aspects" which has already been referred to. This, I hope to show, is not a logical or adequate explanation. I cannot at this time refer more particularly to his argument, as it would be anticipating what will necessarily follow.[1]

In the next chapter we shall consider the nature of the problem to be solved and the difficulties surrounding it.

---

[1] I regret that I should have overlooked the writings of the late Professor Clifford on this subject. It was not till a short time before going to press, and some years after this work was written, that I became aware of his essay, entitled " Body and Mind" (Lectures and Essays). The essay just referred to, together with two others on the same subject, " Things in Themselves" and " The Unseen Universe," are masterpieces of lucid exposition. Professor Clifford, whose death was such a loss to the world, possessed to a rare degree the faculty of both clearly conceiving what he wished to say, and saying it in a happy way that was at once thoroughly intelligible and attractive.

I rejoice to say that the views of this vigorous thinker on the question of the relation between Mind and Body agree with those expressed in this work. He is the only writer so far as I know whose views coincide with those herein advanced. I regret that I am prohibited from referring more particularly in the text to his writings.

# CHAPTER II.

## THE TRUE NATURE OF THE PROBLEM TO BE SOLVED.

HAVING now become familiar with that doctrine which has been most generally accepted by those best qualified to judge, and having seen how far short it falls of explaining the connection between those activities we call mental and those activities we call physical; nay, having seen that it has even been declared that " the task of transcending or abolishing the radical antithesis between the phenomena of mind and the phenomena of motions of matter must always remain an impracticable task. For in order to transcend or abolish this radical antithesis, we must be prepared to show how a given quantity of molecular motion in nerve-tissue can become transformed into a definable amount of ideation or feeling. But this, it is quite safe to say, can never be done;"[1] having become conversant with all this, we shall now proceed, refusing to accept this verdict, to attempt the task; with what success we shall leave to the reader to determine.

I shall state at the outset that theorem which I conceive will answer all the requirements of the case and which it shall be my effort to prove.

It is this: instead of there being one substance with

---

[1] Fiske's Cosmic Philosophy, ii. p. 442.

28

*two properties* or " aspects,"—mind and motion,—*there
is one substance, mind;* and the other *apparent* property, motion, is only the way in which this real substance, mind, is apprehended by a *second organism:*
only the sensations of, or effect upon, the second organism, when acted upon (ideally) by the real substance,
mind.

This may, at first sight, appear to the reader as
practically the same thing, only expressed in different
terms. But it is not so. There is a radical difference
in the conception. The one recognizes one substance
with duality of " properties" or " aspects;" the other,
one substance with one aspect only. If the meaning
of this, at this time, be not clear or be not admitted, I
must ask the reader to suspend his judgment, and to
follow me with open-mindedness through the next
chapter. If it shall then be found that this theorem
both explains all the difficulties we have encountered
and does not lead to conclusions inconsistent with the
facts, I shall consider that I am justified in my reasoning.

In this problem we have to do with the relationship
between two worlds which are considered to be radically antithetical in their nature,—the world of thought
and feeling, and the world of things. The former is
called subjective, the latter objective. It will be necessary before going further to inquire more intimately
into what we mean by each. This inquiry will necessarily involve what will probably be judged by those
learned in the matter a tedious restatement of first
principles, but it is absolutely necessary for a proper
appreciation of the argument for those not well versed

in philosophic matters.   Therefore no apology will be offered for the digression.

The subjective world is well known to every one. We all know what a thought is, or an emotion of fear, or anger, or a sensation of pain or sweetness.   No definition can make the knowledge any more definite. But the objective world about us is not so well known to us.   He who imagines that the things about him in the room—the chairs, the table, the pictures—are really what they seem, is grievously mistaken.   He who picks up a book, and, perceiving something which has a certain shape, size, hardness and color, say redness, and thinks that these qualities reside as such in the something he calls a book, does not know what perceiving a thing consists in.   Physiology teaches us that the qualities of any object, as the book, are only a number of sensations, and accordingly states of our own consciousness.   These sensations we are in the habit of projecting outside of us, and then imagining they exist as such independent of our own consciousness; but as a matter of fact they do not exist as such. When these sensations occur grouped together in a particular way, we call the group, after being thus imagined to exist outside our minds, an object.   Each sensation then becomes a quality of the object which is the whole group.

The object, then, does not exist as such outside of us, but is only a bundle of our sensations.   Undoubtedly something exists outside of us which is the cause of these sensations in us.   This something has been called the thing-in-itself, but its nature is unknown to us. If this is not clear, perhaps an example will make it

so.   We are looking at the question now entirely from
a physiological point of view.   When I say that my
pipe is yellow, I do not mean that there is anything
like yellowness existing in the pipe-itself, but the rays
of light reflected from the "pipe" fall upon the retina,
and a commotion is excited among the fibres of the
optic nerve.   This commotion is conveyed to the brain,
and there, in some way or other (which it will be our
object to explain later), the sensation of yellowness is
created ; so that the quality of yellowness exists in the
mind of the observer and not in the pipe itself.   All
the other qualities of the pipe may similarly be resolved into states of our own consciousness, as, for example, hardness, shape, etc.   It is only after we have
imagined these sensations to exist outside of us that
we can regard the pipe to exist as a pipe at all.   But
after we have abstracted these qualities from the
"pipe," what remains behind?   We have every reason
to believe that something, which we may call the thing-
in-itself, exists independent of our consciousness.   What
this is is another question, which is far beyond our purpose to consider here.   We may simply say that there
are certain activities existing outside our consciousness, which correspond to certain modes of our consciousness, and constitute the *reality* of the latter when
these are projected outside of us to form phenomena.
The nature of these activities is practically unknown
to us.   The only thing we know is our sensations.
The material world is thus resolved into certain unknown activities and certain groups of sensations,
which latter constitute our perception of the former.

That these activities, constituting the thing-in-itself,

exist at all is an inference, but an inference of such irresistible force that we cannot resist it. Thus, the properties of objects are all sensations dependent on unknown activities outside of us. When these activities exist grouped together in a particular way, so as to produce a particular group of sensations, we call this group a book, or table, or chair, and artificially locate the sensations in the external matter as its qualities. These activities in matter, which may be said to constitute matter, are unknown, and should be denominated simply by $\times$.

The application of all this will soon become apparent, if it is not so already. That which we call the subjective world is composed of our thoughts and feelings; that which we call the objective world is a mass of activities unknown to us, but conventionally designated by subjective terms of sensation, as red, hard, sweet, etc.; and these *sensations are the reaction of the organism to these external unknown activities.*

Now to extend this reasoning to the same conditions, but submitted to a further analysis, what do we mean by motions, undulations, and such phenomena? On analyzing light by physical methods we find it to consist of oscillations of molecules of the ether. We find that difference in the color of light is due to a difference in the length of these oscillations; that in red light, for example, the length of oscillation is 0.0000271 inch, and blue light 0.0000155 inch, or a little over half as long as that of the red. Sound is said to be due to vibrations of the atmosphere, and the pitch of any note depends upon the rate of vibration of each particle of air, the greater the rapidity of the vibrations the higher the note, and *vice versa.* Heat is said to be motion among the molecules of matter,— the more rapid or violent the motion the greater the heat.

Now what is meant by all this? Is there anything really existing outside of us identical with these motions? Do these motions or vibrations really exist as such outside of our own mind? Have, in fact, the oscillations of the ether any more real objective existence than red light or green light? Not at all. We have simply made the really existing, but unknown, activities in matter impress us through different channels; made them appear as motion instead of color; made the disturbances of the atmosphere appear through the sense of sight instead of hearing,—as motion instead of sound; made heat appear through the sense of sight instead of touch,—as motion instead of heat. But the new sensations have no more real objective existence than old and familiar ones. These phenomena have simply been translated from terms of one sense into those of another. Color, sound, and heat have now ceased to be such, and have become motion. These activities can be made by suitable devices to appear to us through several senses; but we must never lose sight of the device, nor of the unknown nature of the activities.

When we talk about matter, then, what do we mean? We may have four different notions, each radically distinct, and unless we bear constantly in mind to which we refer we are liable to be led into confusion of thought.

1st. There is the notion we may have of our own

c

conscious states.   As such without reference to any
thing beyond them, and consisting of groups of sensations, as of the motion of two points (which points may
again be resolved into sensations,—color, shape, etc.).
This motion may be called *subjective matter.*

2d. The notion of the unknown reality, or thing-in-
itself, existing outside of us, and corresponding to these
sensations,—the unknown ×.   This may be called
*actual matter.*

3d. The double notion of both these two classes of
facts and the relation between them.   This embraces
the other two, and is the one which should be particularly kept in view when inquiring into the ultimate
nature of things.

4th. The common idea of matter as employed in
ordinary discourse and in the physical sciences.   In
this sense, matter is made to include our conscious
states (1st notion) after being projected outside of us,
and artificially made to have an active existence as
phenomena or objects.   This may be called *phenomenal
matter.*   This, as has already been explained, is philosophically an erroneous notion, being only an artifice,
but nevertheless one that is necessary for the ordinary
purposes of social life and the pursuit of the physical
sciences.   Here it is of inestimable value, and, in fact,
we could not do without it.   It would be ridiculous,
not only in the every-day use of language, but in our
conceptions employed to carry on the ordinary affairs
of life, to bear any other notion in mind.

In discussing philosophical matters, however, it
should always be remembered that it is only through
an artifice, as Lewes has pointed out, that we have this

conception; but it is an artifice that is indispensable when properly employed.

Now in these different notions embraced by " matter" lies the gist of the whole question under consideration. These are facts which even Macaulay's wonderful school-boy ought to know, though it is to be feared that his education has been sadly neglected in this respect. Certainly every one who has discussed the subject since Berkeley wrote knows them, and yet we continually go on talking about " matter" as if it were perfectly plain what we meant, and it were impossible to misunderstand which of the four notions we had reference to. We take the precaution to analyze the meaning of the term in a sort of prologue to our arguments, discover that it covers at least four different classes of facts, insist upon the importance of the discovery, and straightway apparently forget all about it when we happen to require the term for use. I do not think I speak too strongly in saying that it too often happens that we use the word " matter" regardless of the various interpretations that may be placed upon it, and I venture to say that nine times out of ten, even those who are the most precise in the use of terms, will speak of matter without regard to its being an abstract term, and without proper weight being given to the different facts embraced by it. If interrupted in the flow of their talk, they will with great accuracy explain what we know, but in argument the word is used in the most general manner. Hence often difference of opinion arises simply because of the shifting meaning given to the terms employed. Of course, in speaking in this way of the ambiguous use of this word, I refer only to philosophical discussions. In the physical sciences the term is employed with a special signification, and is well understood.

Let us return now to our subject, and apply what has been learned regarding matter to the motions of the cerebral molecules which are said to accompany consciousness. It is evident that in speaking of the molecular motions occurring in your brain I may refer either to the motion proper, which is my state of consciousness, or I may have reference to the reality actually occurring outside of me and belonging to you, and a part of you. If I refer to the former, I know what it is; it is my sensation. If I refer to the latter, the Reality, the question arises, What is it? Is it unknown, and if not, what is its nature? We will approach this question in another way, which will make its meaning clearer.

Let us consider these physical cerebral activities, and ask from a' purely physical point of view what kind of activities they are. We have reference, of course, only to those activities which are supposed to constitute nerve-force and to underlie all conscious states. Suppose that by a suitable device we could have them presented to us *objectively*, so that we could actually recognize them, how would they appear to us? That would depend upon the sense we employed in perceiving them. We might ideally (as we do when thinking of them) or actually *see* them; they would then appear as motions, oscillations, undulations, or some such movement. We might, by the suitable microphone, *hear* them; they would then appear as musical notes. If our tactile sense were sufficiently developed we might *feel* them; they might then appear as heat. But none of these sensations represent these activities as they really *are*.

Now, to put another hypothetical question, suppose, for a moment, that what they really *are* is consciousness,—that is, a thought or sensation of pain,—how would this sensation of pain *appear* to us if we could apprehend it through our senses, and through the sense of sight in particular (either, of course, ideally or in the brain of another)? The answer is, Only as all other activities in matter appear to us, namely, as motions, undulations, etc. *If, then, these hypothetical conditions were the facts*, it would be easy to understand how mental states can become " transformed" into physical disturbances, and *vice versa*, because there is no *transformation* about it.· *There would be in this case only one thing, mental states, which would appear as physical activities when viewed (ideally) through the senses, as tremors if viewed through sight.* Now have we any reason for believing that the actual activities—these physical activities-in-themselves, as they really are— are a state of consciousness? This it shall be our effort to establish by a series of inferences, the only method of proof open to us for such a problem. If we are successful, it would appear that the reason for the difficulty which has been experienced in conceiving how a sensation can become a physical change lies in not properly perceiving the nature of the problem we are trying to solve. A great deal of thought has been devoted to trying to understand how molecular changes are transformed into consciousness, when in reality there is no transformation at all. Another source of error has arisen from regarding the two classes of facts—the physical and the mental—as two different modes of apprehending, or aspects of the same thing. An artificial parallelism has thus been drawn between them which has only served to increase the difficulty, and has prevented all assimilation of one with the other. To this parallelism so much attention has been devoted that the *mode* by which the parallelism arises has been neglected and an artificial difficulty created.

To show how much stress has been laid on this parallelism and to what difficulties it leads when pushed to an extreme degree will require a momentary digression. That a parallelism exists is true, but it has been exaggerated into a great bugbear, because there has not been constantly and clearly kept in mind *what* is parallel. Phenomena have been made abstractions, abstractions unconsciously made entities, and two lines sharply drawn parallel, which originate and diverge from the same point.

To justify this assertion I shall refer to a very able writer, from whom I have had occasion to quote before. "On such grounds as these," says Mr. Fiske, "I maintain that feeling is not a product of nerve-motion in anything like the sense that it is sometimes the product of heat, or that friction electricity is a product of sensible motions. Instead of entering into the dynamic circuit of correlative physical motions, the phenomena of consciousness stand outside as utterly *alien* and *disparate* phenomena. They stand outside but *uniformly parallel* to that segment of the circuit which consists of neural undulations. The relation between what goes on in consciousness and what goes on simultaneously in the nervous system may best be described as a relation of *uniform concomitance.* I agree with Prof. Huxley and Mr. Harrison that along with every act of consciousness there goes a molecular change in the substance of the brain, involving a waste of tissue. This is not materialism, nor does it alter a whit the position in which we were left by common sense before physiology was ever heard of. Everybody knows that so long as we live on earth the activity of mind as a whole is accompanied by activity of the brain as a whole. What nervous physiology teaches is simply that each particular mental act is accompanied by a particular cerebral act. By proving this the two sets of phenomena, mental and physical, are reduced each to its lowest terms, but not a step is taken toward confounding the one with the other. On the contrary, the keener our analysis the more clearly does it appear that the two can never be confounded. The relation of concomitance between them remains an ultimate and insoluble mystery."[1]

Let us see how much truth there is in all this. On examining the passage critically it will be found to contain three distinct propositions : first, that states of mind are phenomena ; secondly, that states of mind, as feeling and neural undulations, are "utterly alien and disparate in nature;" thirdly, that the relation between them is only one of parallelism and "uniform concomitance." Each of these propositions will require separate consideration.

---

[1] North American Review, Jan.–Feb., 1878. The italics are mine.

To the first we will devote only a few words in this place, as it is liable to involve us in a discussion regarding terms merely.

It may very properly be questioned whether states of mind recognized as subjective can be designated by the same terms used to characterize the physical world. If the former are actualities, as I hope to be able to show strong grounds for believing, and the latter merely symbols of something else, then, though the latter are properly classed as phenomena, or the appearances of things, the former should be classed as the thing-in-itself, or actuality, and not phenomena. To insist upon this exactness in the use of terms may appear to the reader to savor of pedantry. But it is not so. Though it may be of no consequence what terms we use so long as we bear continuously in mind the exact conditions which they represent, still it is almost impossible for even the clearest thinkers to keep the thing represented differentiated mentally from the terms representing it, and in the prolongation of an argument the two become unconsciously confused; so that, though the premises may be exactly defined and true, in the conclusion and especially in corollaries and deductions drawn from these conclusions, errors of great magnitude and serious moment creep in. Just as a slight error at the apex of an angle may be of no consequence, yet with every prolongation of the sides the error becomes amplified. So it is with philosophic discussion. The history of philosophy has been the history of the misuse of terms.

As to the second proposition, that the "phenomena" of consciousness are "utterly alien and disparate" from the phenomena of physical motions, it must rest upon either one or two alternatives.

We have seen before (pp. 30–34) that physical motions have no objective reality or existence as such outside of our own minds; on the contrary, they are subjective sensations, similar to any other mental state, though they be *caused* by some physical change in *actual* matter, and of which they are the symbols. Consequently, being subjective, so far from being utterly "alien and disparate phenomena," physical motions and mental states are of exactly the same nature and class. If to this Mr. Fiske replies, as he undoubtedly would, that he takes the other alternative, and means by "physical motions" simply to *symbolize* the *unknown* physical disturbances of which motion is only a subjective representation,—as he must call them something,—then I answer that he clearly begs the question in asserting that they are "utterly alien and disparate;" for, as he confesses that he does not know and cannot know what these unknown physical changes really *are*, he cannot logically assert whether they *are* or *are not* essentially similar to or different from the "phenomena" of consciousness. If we do not know what they are, what right has any one to declare that both may not be of the same nature; or, at least, do so without strong circumstantial evidence in favor of such a conclusion? But no attempt has ever been made through indirect evidence to establish this conclusion. On the contrary, everything points the other way. To assert without circumstantial evidence that the two classes of phenomena are essentially different, is like maintaining that any object whatever, as this pen with

4*

which these lines are written, has no resemblance to any other object lying at the bottom of the sea, when we have no idea whatsoever of the object that is lying there, or any knowledge of the conditions by which it came and remains there.   Nor can I reconcile this passage with his approval of that portion of Mr. Spencer's argument quoted on pages 446–448, vol. ii., of his " Cosmic Philosophy."

*It is absolutely essential that we should bear in mind at the outset that the physical changes which go along with every act of consciousness are in reality not an undulation or a motion, but an unknown* ✕.

This oversight, which it would appear to be, seems to have arisen from too close attention having been paid to the third proposition, or the parallelism and concomitance of the phenomena.   That the two classes of facts are parallel there can be no doubt; that they are concomitant there can be no doubt.   The same thing may be said of the musical note and the vibrations of the tuning-fork.   They are parallel and concomitant; but concomitance is not the *sole* relation. No one would think of confusing visual vibrations with a musical note; the contrast between them is sharp and defined.   So no one can confuse a feeling of pain with the oscillation of a molecule; they are sharply contrasted ; but it may be shown that one is only a mode of cognizing the other, or rather, the former is the actual activity, the latter the mode by which a second person becomes conscious of its existence.   " Can we, then, think of the subjective and objective activities as the same?" asks Mr. Spencer.   Looking at them simply as activities, and not as phenomena, I unhesitatingly answer, "Yes, we can." "Can the oscillation of a molecule," he continues, "be represented in consciousness side by side with a psychical shock and the two be recognized as one? No effort enables us to assimilate them. That a unit of feeling has nothing in common with a unit of motion becomes more than ever manifest when we bring the two into juxtaposition." Mr. Spencer has here misconceived the nature of the problem he is investigating. Such a question is like asking is a stone a tree, or is sound light.

Whatever view he held regarding the likeness or unlikeness of the activities called feeling to the activities underlying the phenomena called a table, we have no reason to believe they are unlike those activities underlying the phenomena called neural undulations, however different they may be made to appear by artificial means.

If this reasoning be correct, the inference is justifiable that too much attention has hitherto been paid to the phenomena themselves and too little to the activities lying behind them. It must not be inferred from anything that has been said in these pages that any of the writers quoted have not recognized the great truths established by Berkeley regarding the amount that is subjective in that which we call matter. On the contrary, in the pages of Fiske and Spencer and others they are reiterated over and over again. But having been once recognized, they are straightway overlooked on being put into application. This will be considered by some an unwarranted assertion, but I believe it to be borne out by the facts.

# CHAPTER III.

## THE SOLUTION.

WE shall now inquire into the grounds we have for the suspicion that states of mind and neural activities are identical, and if it shall be found that the evidence is sufficiently strong to turn this suspicion into a conviction, we shall proceed to an investigation into the conditions which cause them to appear so strongly contrasted.

The method which we shall employ will be the physiological method, as being the one most conducive to positive results; but the conclusions arrived at will then be submitted to the test of subjective analysis; and if they shall stand this test we shall consider that our theorem has been established.

There are two propositions the acceptance of which is absolutely essential for any discussion of the problem on which we are engaged. These are: first, every state of consciousness has its seat in the brain (or at least in some part of the cerebro-spinal system); and, second, every such state is accompanied, as has been so frequently stated above, by a molecular change in the substance of the brain. The first of these has been so well established that it would be tedious to repeat the proofs of it here. The second has also been accepted on all sides by spiritualists and materialists alike. They may both, then, be considered as outside all matter of con-

troversy.   But now I propose to assume what will not
be so readily granted and will even be totally denied
by some people; nevertheless we have a right to assume
it if only as a basis of investigation.   This is, that not
only is every act of consciousness accompanied by a
molecular change in the substance of the brain, but
that the former is in some way dependent upon the
latter, though we may not know *how*.   This is an inference we have a right, from a *physiological* stand-point,
to make.   Everything in cerebral physiology points towards it.   Everything that points to the existence of
these molecular changes and a concomitance of the two
classes of facts—the objective and subjective—points
to this conclusion.   As physiologists we are entitled to
employ the physical method and study both classes of
facts objectively, and when we do so this conclusion is
inevitably forced upon us.   It would be carrying us
too far out of our way to go into all the physiological
facts upon which this reasoning is based; but they may
be summed up in the following brief statements: We
can have no consciousness without a material substance,
the brain, nor without the activity of the brain.   In-
jure the brain and you destroy consciousness; prevent
the activities from going on and we have no consciousness.   Excite these activities and consciousness appears.
They appear *invariably* side by side.   Alter the conditions of occurrence of the physical changes and an
equivalent alteration occurs in consciousness.   Change
the quality and quantity of the physical changes by
disease and a similar alteration of the quality and
quantity of consciousness appears (delirium, etc.).   Increase the intensity and quantity of physical changes

and a concomitant increase takes place in consciousness. This and much more points to a dependent relation.

The admission of this is not a committal of opinion as to the nature of the dependency. It is consistent even with the belief in a spiritual mind, or with the belief that it never can be discovered *how* the one class of facts is dependent on the other. Whatever view be held regarding this point, from a physiological point of view the conclusion of dependency is justifiable and sound. To be sure, it cannot be established by positive and direct proof, and it depends upon a series of inferences for its support. But it is not for that reason to be discarded. How many things in this world which are accepted as established facts are anything more than inferences? The foundations upon which the sciences of chemistry and physics rest are nothing but inferences. The boasted atom and molecule are nothing but hypothetical existences. The ether, into disturbances of which light has been resolved, has only an inferential existence. The external world, everything about us, the books, the table and the chairs in this room, the human beings and the horses and carriages that pass the window, all animate and inanimate things, the world and the universe itself, have only an existence for us based on our inferences. We only *know* the sensations they produce in us; that there is any matter lying behind these sensations and the cause of them is only an inference, but an inference so strong that no one can deny the truth of it. Furthermore, it is upon a series of inferences similar to those upon which the dependency of mind upon matter is based that half the physiological processes of the body are established. It is by means of a similar series of inferences that the liver-cells are said to secrete bile, the peptic cells pepsin, and the salivary cells saliva.[1] It must also be borne in mind to what a large extent we are dependent upon inferences for most of our daily acts. We do not hesitate to convict a man and send him to the gallows, even though the verdict which convicted him was based on a series of inferences. It is only upon a series of inferences that the physician establishes his diagnosis upon which rests the fate of his patient, and upon inferences the merchant and the speculator risk their fortunes.

Yet there are probably those who will deny the validity of the inference that consciousness depends on physical changes being induced in the cells of the brain. They only see parallel phenomena, with no bond of connection between them. What a mental act *is*, how it is related, if at all, to the concomitant molecular change in the brain, is declared to be an insoluble mystery, and they do not advance one iota beyond the point where the question was left by Descartes over two hundred years ago. How thought can proceed *invariably* side by side with physical change and be unconnected with it, be neither material nor spiritual,[2] is difficult to understand. I confess my inability to comprehend such eclectic reasoning. If we touch a lighted match to a piece of paper we find it invariably burns,

---

[1] I hope no one will imagine, because a simile is here employed, referring to the logical process, that the physiological process is meant, and the brain be supposed to *secrete* thought.

[2] Compare Mr. Fiske's assertion that his views are " not materialism" with his argument for quasi-spiritualism in " Cosmic Philosophy," vol. ii. part iii. chap. iv.

consequently we say the cause of the paper burning is
the lighted match. Whenever the gastric cells are
stimulated gastric juice is formed. We still say that
the latter is dependent upon the former. But in the
brain a sharp line is drawn. Though mental activity
is invariably connected with cell activity, no dependent
relation is admitted by some. It is difficult to appre-
ciate the consistency in asserting the one and denying
the other. I think we have as much reason in the one
case as in the other, so long as we deal with physiological inquiries, in holding that one group of phenomena
is dependent upon the other group, though we may not
understand *how* it is so dependent. If one chooses to
deny the validity of all causes on the ground that we
only know sequence in time, and that the idea of cause
and effect is only an abstraction of the mind, all well
and good. But if cause is admitted in one case, it must
be in the other also.[1]

It is only so long as we study the problem from a
physiological stand-point that we observe two processes,
—the physical and the mental. The minute we leave
physiology we find that there are not two processes, but
only one process, and a feeling is not strictly accompanied by a physical change. This will soon be shown.

There is one amusing thing connected with this discussion, and that is the readiness with which those
who deny any relationship between the mental and
physical phenomena seize upon the theory of a physical substratum to consciousness and maintain the existence of physical changes " in the substance of the

---

[1] It may be thought that I am arguing against imaginary objections. If so, no harm is done.

brain involving a waste of tissue," and which " go along with every act of consciousness." This doctrine they maintain with a confidence that is amazing, considering that it is entirely beyond the possibility of so-called proof. It is in reality only theory, and supported merely by a series of inferences similar to those upon which the doctrine maintained here is based. Neither less nor more. And yet it is commonly stated as if it were an established fact, entirely beyond cavil, and that, too, by the very persons who refuse to recognize the force of a similar process of reasoning to establish a relationship between mental and physical phenomena. But I do not wish to be understood to push the ground from under my own feet. There is every reason to believe that these physical changes do occur, and that they are the foundation of every doctrine of a physical basis of mind. But they cannot be considered as absolutely established, and rest simply on evidence similar to that for the theory advocated in these pages.

To proceed with our argument. We have two classes of facts, mental and physical ; the former we assume[1] to be dependent upon the latter. The one we know as thought, sensation, and emotion ; the other utterly unknown objectively, but represented by symbols in consciousness. What is the nature of this dependence ? There are four possibilities, and four only, which are thinkable.

*First.* Consciousness may be formed, secreted, manufactured, so to speak, by the protoplasmic activity of

---

[1] If any one denies the validity of this assumption, but admits the rest of my logic, I am amply satisfied. The case is then sufficiently proved.

the cells of the brain, after the same manner that liver-cells secrete bile.

*Second.* Consciousness may be a change in the mutual relations of the *actual* or *real* molecules of the protoplasm of the brain-cells; that is, *these unknown physical disturbances themselves,—the protoplasmic disturbances as they really are; the actuality of so-called neural undulations.* It would possibly be equivalent to the *passage* of the protoplasm from a higher to a lower state of chemical combination, or more probably some physical as opposed to a chemical change, as, say, so-called undulations or vibrations.

*Third.* It may be the essence or actuality of a second and parallel physical change in the protoplasm. Supposing, for example, the physical change, which enters into the nervous circuit, beginning at one end as irritations, and ending at the other in muscular action, to be undulations in nervous matter, consciousness might then be the actuality of a second physical change induced by the parallel and concomitant physical change.

*Fourth.* Consciousness may be the reality of a change induced by the cerebral molecules in a second substance pervading all matter (and therefore the brain), the ether.

A very little consideration will show that the *first* of these propositions is not only untenable, but may be reduced to an absurdity. It would not be seriously considered here were it not that an expression made use of by a German physiologist has given rise, rightly or wrongly, to the idea that such an explanation has been maintained as a doctrine of materialism. According to this view, every thought must be something new-formed, something newly brought into existence. But this something must be either *immaterial* or *material.* In the former case, aside from the inconceivable conception of a material substance manufacturing an immaterial or spiritual thing or entity, it becomes necessary to revive the old doctrine of a supernatural or spiritual mind. This in itself is a sufficient objection. I shall have more to say in regard to it later. In the latter case, if this new-formed substance, a thought or idea is a material something, it necessarily follows that this secretion, for such it must be, must remain (*a*) in the brain; or (*b*) be removed as such by the natural channels, the blood- and lymph-vessels; or (*c*) be decomposed soon after formation, leaving its resulting products to be removed. The objections to, or rather the absurdity of, all these possibilities (or impossibilities) is so obvious, that any serious discussion of them seems unnecessary. But it is somewhat startling to think of the peril in which the life of any individual, who boasts of an abundance of ideas, would be placed from the accumulation of this extraordinary secretion beneath the skull. One can imagine that the effect would be similar to filling his head with dried peas, and then pumping it full of water. The sword of Damocles would be a mere bagatelle compared to the danger of his own thoughts. Like a steam-engine without a safety-valve, he would be the generator of the power that would explode himself. While if his ideas and sensations were removed as such, by the vessels, they would be carried away to all parts of his body whithersoever the blood and lymph flowed. We might then be said **literally** to carry our ideas in our finger-tips, while our inner organs would once more be embellished with our emotions and the peculiarities of our character,—a sort of visceral phrenology. We might, with literal truth, be said to have " bowels of compassion," and to have a " heart full of feeling."

The *third* hypothesis is not so easily disposed of, and yet it will not be difficult to show that it is untenable. In the first place, it leads to the negation of consciousness as a causative factor in all our action. It makes consciousness superfluous, as everything could be done as well without consciousness as with it. Consciousness becomes the steam-whistle to the engine. This was shown in the first chapter. It reduces the doctrine to an absurdity.

In the second place, it is incompatible with the doctrine of the correlation of forces; for, if those physical activities called neural vibrations enter as links in the dynamic circuit, which begins with the ingoing current and ends with the outgoing current, there is no link left for those activities called mental. (See page 16, also Chap. V.)

In the third place, it is an unnecessary and superfluous element. If consciousness could be identical with these second physical activities, so could it be with the first series of activities. There is nothing in favor of the former that does not speak for the latter, which are included in the second hypothesis.

The *fourth* proposition,[1] that mind is the *Reality* of

---

[1] I scarcely imagined when this chapter was written, some eight or nine years ago, that those *unknown* activities, represented to us objectively as the ether, would ever be seriously proposed as an explanation of the nature of mind, and much less

a molecular change transmitted to the ether, is also one which cannot be maintained. It is open to every objection to which the third is subject. These objections are fatal to it. As with the second activities so with the ether. We gain nothing by transferring this disturbance to a second substance, about which we know

---

that the ether in its *material* aspect would be so made use of. But such seems to have been the case. Dr. Maudsley, in a work lately published (Body and Will, Kegan, Paul & Co., 1883), utilizes the ether as a means of bridging over the conventional chasm between mind and matter, and as explaining what mind is. "Perhaps . . . the theory of an all-pervading mentiferous ether," he says, "may help to bridge over the difficulty. For if the object and the brain are alike pervaded by such a hypersubtile ether; and if the impressions which the particular object makes upon the mind be then a sort of pattern of the mentiferous undulations as they are stirred and conditioned within it by its particular form and properties; and *if the mind in turn be the mentiferous undulations* [italics are mine] as conditioned by the convoluted form and the exceedingly complicated and delicate structure of the brain; then it is plain that we have eluded the impassable difficulty of conceiving the action of mind upon matter—the material upon the immaterial—which results from the notion of their entirely different natures. Here, in fact, is a theory that gets rid at the same time of the gross materiality of matter and of the intangible spiritualities of mind, and instead of binding them together in an abhorred and unnatural union of opposites, unites them in a happy and congenial marriage in an intermediate substance,—a substance which, mediator-like, partakes of the nature of both without being exclusively either." The fallacies, only out of respect for Dr. Maudsley's ability I do not say absurdities, of such an hypothesis must be apparent to the reader who has followed me thus far. The fact that such a crude notion could be seriously entertained by a writer having such a special knowledge of the subject as Dr. Maudsley, shows how little understood must be even the nature of the problem with which we are dealing.

scarcely anything, save a certain amount of mystery, while we break the Newtonian canon, forbidding us to postulate new causes before proving the inadequacy of existing ones.  If consciousness can be produced by atoms of ether, in a state of change, why cannot it be done by atoms of protoplasm under similar conditions? Furthermore, the introduction of a new factor brings with it new difficulties which are quite as troublesome to explain.  For instance, it is very difficult to understand how changes in a homogeneous substance, such as we must understand the ether to be, can give rise to the multitude of heterogeneous ideas and sensations of which the human mind is possessed, unless there be a different kind of change for every species of mental progress; a most improbable, if not impossible, assumption.  But, supposing it to be the case, these heterogeneous disturbances of the ether must be indicated by corresponding changes in the protoplasm of the brain; in which case the ether, from a logical point of view, would be an entirely unnecessary factor, and hence there is no necessity for introducing it as an element in the problem.

We are left, then, with the second hypothesis, against which none of the objections to the others obtain.  According to this, consciousness is the unknown cerebral activities underlying the phenomena which we call neural disturbances or motions.  It may be called an alteration in the temporary conditions under which the Realities of the atoms of protoplasm of the brain exist. Consciousness is the supposed "unknown" disturbances X, which in this case are known to us.  It is the actual physical change as it *really* occurs, not as it appears to us objectively. It may be called the essence of physical change in cerebral protoplasm. In other words, *a mental state and those physical changes which are known in the objective world as neural undulations are one and the same thing,* BUT THE FORMER IS THE ACTUALITY, THE LATTER A MODE BY WHICH IT IS PRESENTED TO THE CONSCIOUSNESS OF A SECOND PER-SON,[1]—*i.e.,* to the non-possessor of it.

Having arrived at this apparently paradoxical conclusion, the task still remains to us to explain the sole objection which can be urged against it, and this is: How does it happen that cerebral activity or consciousness can be presented to us under such strongly contrasted forms? This will be considered by some persons to be the same thing as the original problem, How physical changes or matter becomes transformed into consciousness; but with the foregoing presentation of the problem it has assumed another aspect. The real question is, not regarding the transformation of matter into mind, but how *one state of consciousness comes to be perceived as another state of consciousness,* or how a subjective fact comes to be perceived as an objective fact; how a feeling comes to be presented to us as a vibration.

Unless this can be satisfactorily answered, the conclusion at which we have just arrived cannot claim acceptance. For this purpose it will be necessary to submit it to subjective analysis, as was promised at the outset; and after this has been done, if we find that

---

[1] It is not sufficiently exact to say that *both* are different modes of apprehending one and the same thing, for that implies that neither is the actuality. See Chapter IV.

there is no real contradiction, we shall consider that
our theorem has been established.

For those who are accustomed to think on such matters what has already been said in the last chapter will
be sufficient, and they will see at once that there is no
real difficulty; but for the majority of readers some
further explanation will be necessary.

Whether the explanation which has already been
suggested, and will now be offered with more detail,
will prove as satisfactory to others as to the writer remains to be seen.   The confidence of the writer in its
adequacy and correctness is naturally strengthened by
the fact that though arrived at independently by him
many years ago, it is in many points similar to that
originally offered by Mr. Lewes, to whom the credit is
due for having been the first to really perceive the true
nature of the problem.   It almost seems, if the reasoning here employed is correct, as if Mr. Lewes, however,
had missed the point of his argument, for he expresses
his conclusions in terms which do not seem to the writer
to be applicable.   He considers the difference between
the mental and the physical processes to be one of
aspects, and to be dependent upon the difference in the
modes of apprehension.   My objection to this mode of .
expressing the relationship will be given later.   The
difference between us may be only one of terms; but
as Mr. Lewes himself has most rigorously insisted on
the necessity of precision in the use of terms, I have
less hesitation in calling attention to the distinction.[1]

---

[1] The late Prof. Clifford is the only writer, so far as I know,
whose views on the relation of the mind to matter thoroughly
coincide with those herein expressed.

It may at first sight appear impossible that these physical phenomena, with which we are familiar, as motion, undulations, or what you will, can also appear as states of consciousness. But this is because in our daily experience we are apt to overlook the well-known fact, which has been sufficiently explained in the preceding chapter, that all those properties with which we endow matter have no objective existence, but are only subjective states called sensations, and hence forms of consciousness, and these are symbolic only of the unknown change occurring in matter. Just as the words written on this page are symbolic of the ideas they represent, but are as unlike as possible the ideas themselves. Any sensation, such as light, is a representation in consciousness of physical changes in matter outside the brain, but gives us no idea what those changes are. A sensation is related to its physical external cause as the dent in the hot iron is to the blow of the blacksmith's hammer that fashions it. The true nature of a physical change in a foreign body—a piece of iron, for example—is absolutely beyond our range of comprehension. A physical change in my brain is an idea, my idea. To you, could you in some way become conscious of it, it would appear only like any other physical phenomenon,—as, for instance, a vibration,—being only symbolized in your consciousness; and when you ideally conceive it, it is not the idea itself which you are conscious of, but the disturbance in your brain in the form of a sensation, and this you characterize as a physical phenomenon, and locate in mine. So that a disturbance in my brain which I experience as an idea of an orange, you *ideally* experience as a physical phenomenon in the form of a neural undulation or some similar (objective) sensation.

Let us take a concrete example. We will imagine that you have a sensation of pain presented to your mind; we will also picture to ourselves a physical process in your brain in the form of neural vibrations. Now these two—the mental and physical—are usually described as two processes, both of which occur somehow in you. They are said to take place synchronously, and one is the correlate of the other. But this is not the correct way of putting it. We will suppose now, further, I could apply a microscope to your brain and watch the cells (as I can *ideally*) when this pain is felt by you. What now would happen? At the moment when *you* have the sensation of *pain I* become conscious of *neural vibrations*, which I locate as such (but erroneously) in your brain-cells. The real activities in you are pain, not neural vibrations. The reason for this is this: your mental process, the pain, acting upon my retina sets up a process in me, and as this process of mine is excited through my organ of vision, I am affected according to the physiological laws of this organ and become conscious of neural vibrations. These neural vibrations I erroneously locate in you while they really are parts of my consciousness, and the only thing which occurs in you is the feeling of *pain*. The reaction of my brain to your feeling is a sensation of vibrations. The only way in which these activities could be apprehended by me is objectively as neural vibrations. The only way in which they can be brought into your consciousness is as the sensation of pain. But, in fact, it is one process in you, the sensation of pain, which is

the real activity. Here, then, lies the parallelism of
the phenomena: *your* consciousness or pain is the correlate of *my* apprehension of this consciousness as neural vibration. *The parallelism is between your consciousness and my consciousness of your consciousness, or, what
is the same thing, between the consciousness in you and the
picture in my mind of neural vibrations.* The former is
the reality, the latter the symbol of it. There is an
invariable concomitance of these facts.

Again, under the hypothetical conditions stated
above, I cannot become conscious of your physical
changes or process in its true form, the sensation of
pain, for that which I become conscious of is the *effect*
which this physical process produces in my brain, the
reaction of my brain to it, as a sensation of neural
vibrations. To be sure, I can conjure up the sensation of pain by allowing my mind to dwell on it,
and produce in this way a so-called imaginary pain;
but this is an entirely different thing. In that
case there would be no relation between *my* mental
state of pain and *your* mental state, which I am endeav-
oring to become conscious of. So you can picture to
yourself neural vibrations as well as I, and perceive
them as objective phenomena. But here, too, the conditions are altered, and we have to do not with a mental
process and its correlated neural process, but with a
physical process ideally projected outside of your cerebrum, and a symbolic representation of it as neural
vibrations in your mind.

It is no objection to this statement of the nature of
the parallelism to say that there is something more
than a parallelism between your consciousness and my

mode of becoming conscious of your consciousness, because you can have both consciousness as pain and a picture of neural vibrations supposed to occur side by side with the former, for this amounts to the same thing. For when you conceive of correlated neural processes in your brain you in reality have gone through the following logical process : you first have perceived hypothetical physical disturbances in some one else's brain, and these you have recognized as neural vibrations. Then you have inferred that they occur invariably side by side with the consciousness of the individual. Having determined this, you ideally abstract them, transfer them to your own brain, and infer that they occur there under similar conditions. This is the same thing as if a second individual had been the object of your study. Then it follows that when you think of physical changes in the protoplasm of your brain you ideally abstract and project them outside of you, and then ideally become conscious of the *effect* which they produce on your mind, namely, the sensation of vibrations; but this *effect* is entirely distinct in character from, though correlative with, the ideas which are the realities.

*Physical changes occurring in a foreign body, as a piece of iron, though giving us our experience of it, must be absolutely unknown to us. Physical changes occurring in our brains are clearly known to us; they are our thoughts, our sensations, and our emotions.*

# CHAPTER IV.

## THE NATURE OF THE MIND.

FROM this point of view it is plainly evident how barren must be the question, What is the *ultimate* nature of mind? when by it is meant a desire to go behind the facts of consciousness. The very question involves an absurdity. We all know what mind is by direct consciousness. Mind is mind and that is the end of it. When we step on a needle and feel pain we know what pain is; and if we could resolve it into a dozen physical elements, such as vibrations among those molecules which make up the protoplasm of the brain-cells, it would give us no new information on the nature of pain. Those vibrations are not pain, but every one knows what pain is. When we are angry with any one for an injury done us, or feel sorrow at the death of a friend, we know what sorrow and anger are. The mere consciousness of these emotions is sufficient. So we all know what the idea of a horse is. When we say these different mental states are molecular vibrations in nervous matter, it is, as Lewes has well pointed out, a mere artifice to enable us to study the conditions under which these states of consciousness are generated. This artifice is of inestimable value; but the fact must never be lost sight of that it is an artifice, and the artifice must never be con-

founded with the reality, which is the mental state.
When the physicist declares that light is a vibration
of the ether, and the chemist that sulphate of iron is
green and sulphide of lead is black, both make use of
a similar artifice, and endow matter with properties
which exist only in their own minds. This is a device
which is not only justifiable but necessary for the study
of nature and the progress of science. In no other
way could we examine the conditions under which
phenomena exist, and determine relations of difference
and agreement, in which all knowledge of the objective world consists. It is so with the study of mind
when we employ the physiological method. When we
study mental states as physical conditions we use the
physiological method ; but when we inquire into the
*ultimate nature* of things, and desire to know more of
mind than is furnished by consciousness, we fail to
bear in mind what knowing a thing consists in.
When we ask what water is, the chemist tells us it
is composed of hydrogen and oxygen. But hydrogen
and oxygen are not water: it is only when they are
chemically united that we have water, and then we
have hydrogen and oxygen as such no longer. When
we ask what sound is, the physicist says it is the vibration of air. But have we now any more intimate
knowledge of its essential nature? On the contrary,
sound is the sensation which is the effect of certain
unknown disturbances in matter acting on our auditory apparatus; and when we describe these disturbances as vibrations we artificially make them appear to
us through sight, and simply transfer them from terms
of one sense into those of another. We seem to know

them better because the sensations of sight are usually
more vivid and complex than those of sound. It is
the same with heat. Neither sound nor vibrations nor
heat are the real disturbances. These must be forever *unknown* to us. Knowing the *nature* of a thing,
then, in the objective world merely consists in trans-
lating the terms of perception from those of one sense
into those of another, or into different terms of the
same sense. How, then, can we have a more intimate
knowledge of the nature of mind by saying it is neural
vibrations? We might, by means of an extraordinarily
delicate microphone, listen to the murmur of the molecules as they jingle against one another in the myriads
of cells of the brain. In that case it might be said
that mind was a musical note. Actual feeling is not
molecular vibration, though it may be presented to our
senses as such; but there is no objection to our using
physical terms to describe states of consciousness if we
keep in mind the object we have in view, any more
than there is to the physicist's using terms of sight to
describe phenomena of sound. In both cases they
answer the same purposes.

But further, let us suppose that these physical disturbances could be shown to be vibrations in nervous
protoplasms, and that we could actually see them under
the microscope. Would we now have any better
knowledge of the ultimate nature of mind than at
present,—aside from the fact, of course, of the physical
motions having been demonstrated? I hold not. Why
should the seeker after the ultimate nature of things be
content to rest satisfied with these? He should logically ask, " What is the ultimate nature of vibrations?"

and the answer to this would bring him back again to where he started, for he would be told that they were mind. Consciousness I conceive to be an ultimate, at least as far as physical processes are concerned, and hence the question as to its further ultimate nature must be an absurdity. This point, as well as the subject-matter of the last chapter, has been dwelt upon at the expense of considerable repetition because of the importance of clearly recognizing what we mean by mind. When thus viewed, we get rid of the difficulty of conceiving how a mental and a physical process can be one and the same thing, and how a transition is effected between the physical change in the body and the subjective world of thought,—the passage between mind and body. This has been a difficulty which has been a stumbling-block in the way of all schools of philosophy, both spiritual and material. It matters not whether mind be a spirit or a manifestation of matter, the difficulty has been found the same. This has already been pointed out. Even so advanced a writer as Dr. Carpenter, a writer of the physiological school, makes this admission. "Now in what way," he says, "the *physical* change thus excited in the sensorium is translated, so to speak, into that *psychical* change which we call *seeing* the object whose image was found upon our retina, we know nothing whatever." [1] Ferrier recognizes a similar puzzle, but just misses grasping what, I think, must eventually be recognized as the true solution.

"*But how it is that molecular changes in the brain-*

---

[1] Mental Physiology, p. 13.

*cells coincide with modifications of consciousness;* how, for instance, the vibrations of light falling on the retina excite the modifications of consciousness termed a visual sensation is a problem which cannot be solved. We may succeed in determining the exact nature of the molecular changes which occur in the brain-cells when a sensation is experienced, but this will not bring us one whit nearer the ultimate nature of that which constitutes the sensation. The one is objective, the other subjective, and neither can be expressed in terms of the other. *We cannot say that they are identical, or even that the one passes into the other;* but only as Laycock expresses it, that the two are correlated, or with Bain, that the physical changes and the psychical modifications are the objective and subjective sides of a double-faced unity."[1] Even such an extreme materialist as Büchner, who has been more soundly abused for his writings than any other materialist of the age by people, who either could not, or more generally would not, understand him, does not even attempt to explain the connection between mind and matter. He contents himself with merely stating the existence of the connection. This connection becomes apparent now that the problem is found really to be not how molecular changes become transformed into consciousness, but how consciousness comes to be apprehended as physical changes. If the views that have been advocated above are accepted, this can readily be understood. It must be distinctly understood that it is not a question of translation or *transformation* at all, but of *identification.*

---

[1] The Functions of the Brain, 1876. The italics are mine.

Physical changes are not transformed into states of consciousness, nor are there "two processes" which occur "side by side" in the same person. *There is only one process.*

The common expression that "every state of consciousness is accompanied with a molecular change in the substance of the brain," which was for the sake of argument provisionally accepted in the preceding pages, *must be regarded as unfounded and as leading to great confusion and misconception. A feeling is* NOT *accompanied by a molecular change in the same brain; it is "the reality itself of that change."* You may say, if you prefer, that a feeling in you may be ideally perceived by me as a molecular change, or that your feeling is ideally accompanied by my notion of molecular changes. *But you cannot correctly say that a feeling is accompanied by a molecular change in the same organism, because this implies two distinct existences and leads to all the fallacies of materialism.*

"It is not only inconceivable," writes Mr. Fiske, "*how* mind should have been produced from matter, but it is inconceivable *that* it should have been produced from matter, unless matter possessed already the attributes of mind in embryo, an alternative which it is difficult to invest with any real meaning."[1]

Here we have a capital illustration of the ambiguous use of the word matter; for when we clearly define to ourselves in which sense we employ the term the difficulty vanishes. Does Mr. Fiske here refer to subjective, actual, or phenomenal matter?[2] Not, cer-

---

[1] North Am. Rev., Jan.-Feb., 1878.　　　[2] See page 33.

tainly, to the first, for *subjective* matter being a form of mind the statement loses all force, as it becomes equivalent to saying that mind could not have been produced from mind.

If by matter is meant *phenomenal* matter, the proposition is undoubtedly correct, for phenomenal matter, being only the product of an artifice, has no real existence. But with this admission it is difficult to see much point to the statement, as I do not know as any one has ever imagined that phenomenal matter could produce mind. The supposition is mere nonsense, being equivalent to saying that something which does not exist can produce something that does.

· Finally, if by matter Mr. Fiske has in mind the notion of *actual* matter, then the proposition assumes an intelligible meaning, but at the same time can readily be shown to be untrue. By actual matter we mean the unknown reality underlying phenomena, the thing-in-itself. It comprises all those unknown forces or activities which constitute the essence of the universe. If it is unknown, then we certainly are precluded from setting limitations to its possibilities. It may be inconceivable *how* mind should have been produced from this great unknown universe, because such a conception would require an intimate knowledge of the nature of that which, by its very definition, is unknown. But, on the other hand, nothing forbids our conceiving *that* mind should be produced from such a universe; and the alternative, that in this case matter must have possessed the attributes of mind in embryo, instead of being devoid of meaning, becomes invested with the deepest signification. It is not only possible, but in the highest degree probable, that those activities, the sum of which we call consciousness, are of a kindred nature to those activities which are the reality of phenomenal matter.    Just as organic matter is made up of the same physical atoms and molecules which make up inorganic matter, combined and recombined in varying proportions, so there is every reason to believe that states of consciousness are the resultant of the combination and recombination of the elementary activities which are the realities of the physical atoms and molecules.    The atom of hydrogen is the same, whether it occur in a free state by itself or combined with two atoms of oxygen in the form of water, or with a great many other atoms of carbon, nitrogen, oxygen, and hydrogen in the living organic substance called protoplasm ; and there is also every reason to believe that the " force," if we may employ a term which derives its signification from our experience to denote that of which we have no experience,—there is every reason to believe, I say, that the force, which is the reality of the hydrogen atom, is the same whether that atom be in a free state, or in water, or in living protoplasm. Further, as the different combinations of the forces or Realities lying behind the atoms of inorganic substances exhibit themselves in the varying properties of such substances, so the various and more complicated combinations of the same forces in living protoplasm exhibit themselves in its properties or vital functions.    By a still further combination of the activities underlying the properties of the simplest form of living substance, a lump of protoplasm, and manifesting themselves in its vital functions, the primitive germs of consciousness arise, and we obtain for the first time a glimpse of what these forces of the unknown universe may be.[1] All higher states of consciousness are but combinations of the simpler forms.

---

[1] This identification of the Reality of matter with the elements of consciousness was clearly recognized by Clifford, and set forth by him with that brilliant felicity of expression and clearness of conception which was pre-eminently his.

This Reality he calls mind-stuff. "That element," he says, "of which, as we have seen, even the simplest feeling is a complex, I shall call *mind-stuff*. A moving molecule of inorganic matter does not possess mind or consciousness; but it possesses a small piece of mind-stuff. When molecules are so combined together as to form a film on the under side of a jelly-fish, the elements of mind-stuff which go along with them are so combined as to form the faint beginnings of sentience." Again; "The universe, then, consists entirely of mind-stuff. Some of this is woven into the complex form of human minds containing imperfect representations of the mind-stuff outside of them, and of themselves, as a mirror reflects its own image in another mirror *ad infinitum*. Such an imperfect representation is called a material universe. It is a picture in a man's mind of the real universe of mind-stuff. The two chief points of this doctrine may be thus summed up:

"Matter is a mental picture in which mind-stuff is the thing represented.

"Reason, intelligence, volition are properties of a complex which is made up of elements themselves not rational not intelligent, not conscious." *Things-in-themselves.*

Mr. Spencer seems also to have come round to this idea, and clearly expressed it in a late article, which has given rise to considerable discussion. "Consequently," he says, "the final outcome of that speculation commenced by the primitive man is that the power manifested throughout the universe distinguished as material, is the same power which in ourselves wells up under the form of consciousness."—*Religion—a Retrospect and Prospect. Nineteenth Century*, Jan., 1884.

Thus it becomes intelligible how matter, meaning thereby *actual* matter, may possess the "attributes of mind in embryo." But such use of language is metaphorical, and is justifiable only on the recognition of the fact that it is metaphor we are using.

But after admitting that consciousness is the reality of physical processes, the question may be asked; Is there still something more underlying consciousness, some substance of which consciousness may be (as Mr. Spencer holds) a mode or manifestation? Mr. Spencer's view, I take it, is that consciousness is not the reality of physical processes, but an aspect or manifestation of this reality. This reality he then calls the substance of mind, and argues that it is the unknown.

I confess that after a careful and patient study of Mr. Spencer's arguments I am unable to admit their force.

Grant the existence of this substance of mind, and it necessarily follows, as he has so ably argued, that we can know nothing of it. But what is this hypothetical "Substance of mind," and what are its relations, on the one hand, to the cerebral vibrations which "underlie thought," and, on the other, to Thought itself? The minute we ask these questions and seek for answers that will enable us to form a clear conception of what sort of part this substance is supposed to play, its mystic nature at once becomes apparent. For any hypothesis to be comprehensive and satisfactory it is essential that we should be able to form a definite and clear picture in our minds of the conditions which we suppose to be present, but I doubt very much whether any one can form such a picture from Mr. Spencer's exposition of the subject, whatever Mr. Spencer's own condition of mind may be. Nay, more, I do not see how different passages in his writings can be reconciled one with another.

In the first place, what evidence can be adduced in favor of this Substance. "Let us yield," he says, "to the necessity of regarding impressions and ideas as forms or modes of a continually existing something. Failing in every effort to break the series of impressions and ideas in two, we are prevented from thinking of them as separate existences. While each particular impression or idea can be absent, that which holds impression and ideas together is never absent, and its unceasing presence necessitates, or indeed constitutes, the notion of continuous existence or reality."

I am unable to see in this more than a subtle playing with thought, if not with words. Admitting that while consciousness is present we cannot have an idea or impression isolated from every other idea or impression, which is, I presume, what is meant by failure to break the series in two, I fail to see this logical necessity which compels us to thus look upon ideas as "modes of a continually existing something" and which prevents us from regarding them as separate existences; or at any rate, whether we do the latter or not depends upon what is meant by existence, a question which, if entered into here, would prolong too far this discussion already grown to great length. The argument also contains a manifest *petitio principii.* "That which holds impressions and ideas together is never absent," it is said. This can only be asserted on the assumption that there *is* something more than and in addition to consciousness, which holds every state of consciousness together. But the only proof of this is the assertion, or a possible inference from our failure " to break the series of ideas and impressions in two ;" an inference which ignores all other possible explanations. The existence of this substance of mind is first assumed, and then said never to be absent. It would not be irrelevant to ask what becomes of this substance during sleep and similar states of unconsciousness, and how it is known that here it is not absent. When we analyze our thoughts, we find that we know only successive and coexisting states of consciousness,—nothing more,—and though we may *infer* there is something more underlying them and holding them together, such a conclusion would be an inference which may or may not be true, and, as Mr. Spencer argues, we can know nothing about its nature whatsoever. It seems somewhat strange, then, that Mr. Spencer should assume that, " by the definition, it [the substance of mind] is that which undergoes the modification producing a state of mind." For, as we can know nothing about it, it would seem evident that we cannot know whether or not it is capable of " undergoing a modification." This seems a curious assumption regarding the qualities of a thing which it is one's endeavor to show is absolutely unknowable, which Mr. Spencer proceeds to do.

But admitting the existence of this substance of mind, what is it, and what are its relations to states of consciousness and to the physical vibrations of the brain ? At first sight it would seem—and this interpretation is most in harmony with other passages in

Mr. Spencer's writings—that the substance of mind is identified with the Unknown Reality lying behind the phenomena of physical motion; so that this great Unknown "Force" is capable of being presented to our consciousness under two forms; namely, when viewed through the senses as physical vibrations, when otherwise viewed (*how?*) as states of consciousness; but in either case the Reality always remains unknown. This seems to be clearly enough meant in the passage, "For what is objectively a change in a superior nerve-centre is subjectively a feeling, and the duration under the one aspect measures the duration of it under the other."[1] And again in the passage, "When with these conclusions that matter and motion, as we think them, are but symbols of unknowable forms of existence, we join the conclusion lately reached that mind also is unknowable, and that the simplest form under which we can think of its substance is but a symbol of something that can never be rendered into thought; we see that the whole question is at least nothing more than the question whether these symbols should be expressed in terms of those, or those in terms of these, a question scarcely worth deciding, since either answer leaves us as completely outside the reality as we were at first."[2] This view of the case is essentially the same as that which was held by Lewes.

The objections to regarding states of consciousness as a mode of apprehending or as symbols of an Unknown Substance will be presently given. I may briefly say here that any such conception makes the relation be-

---

[1] Loc. cit.      [2] Op. cit , p. 159.

tween the states of consciousness we call cerebral motions (subjective matter) and the Unknown Reality (actual matter) similar to the relation between that consciousness which is said to be correlated with those motions and this same Unknown Reality, which is impossible.

But, on the other hand, if this be the intent of Mr. Spencer's position, why should consciousness be regarded as a mode or manifestation of the substance of mind? As has been said, this substance being something far beyond the possibility of our knowledge, we cannot even say it is capable of having modes or manifestation.

The radical distinction between Mr. Spencer's position and mine is this: He supposes an *unknown* Reality, which, when apprehended through the senses, is recognized as physical motions, but which, after having undergone certain modifications, becomes known as mind. (How?)

The view here maintained is that every state of consciousness is not a "mode or manifestation" of an unknown Reality, but is the Reality itself, which is therefore *known*, and which becomes recognized as a physical motion of some kind when apprehended by a second person through the senses.

Mr. Spencer's views have led him to the conclusion that "Though mind and nervous action are the subjective and objective faces of the same thing, we remain utterly incapable of seeing and even imagining how the two are related." On the other hand, the views here maintained show clearly and satisfactorily how the two are related.

Mr. Spencer describes consciousness indifferently as "modes or manifestations," "symbols," and "aspects" of an underlying substance. But no such language can be used to describe the conditions we have endeavored to prove.

In only one sense can there be said to be an Unknown Substance of Mind, and this we can arrive at only by objective inquiry. The molecular motions which correspond to any state of consciousness take place in a very highly organized substance, the protoplasm of the brain-cells. Now this substance is of a very complex composition, being made up of a very great number of atoms of carbon, hydrogen, nitrogen, and oxygen. But to each atom there is a corresponding unknown " force," which is the Reality of it, while the Reality of a *molecule* of protoplasm may be regarded as the result of the combination of Realities of the atoms. Going further, whether we adopt the vortex theory of Thompson or not, as there is reason to believe the atoms of different chemical elements are compounds of some simpler substance, which for the sake of illustration we may call hydrogen, so the Realities of these different chemical atoms will be the combination in varying proportions of the centres of force lying behind the hydrogen atom. The Reality, then, which is the unknown " force" lying behind and corresponding to that group of sensations we call a molecule of cerebral protoplasm, will be a compound of the Realities of its ingredient atoms, which in turn are a compound of the Reality of the primitive (hydrogen ?) atom.

Now as the interaction of the Realities of the protoplasmic molecules constitutes consciousness, we may imagine *different states* or kinds of consciousness to

correspond to the interaction of varying groups of
molecules of the same or different chemical composition, these molecules being contained in a varying
number of cells of the brain.

The Reality, then, of the molecule of protoplasm in
contradistinction to the Reality of the interaction of
the molecules might in this sense be regarded as the
substance of mind, though the same process of reasoning would compel us, perhaps, not to rest here, but to
continue our analysis until we had arrived at the reality
or force underlying the group of sensations called the
atom of hydrogen, or whatever the primitive substance
may be. This would then be the Substance of Mind.

This brings us to another matter which has already
been touched upon, but on which it was promised that
something more would be said. I refer to the matter
of "Aspects." We have seen how physical processes
and consciousness have been spoken of by some as dual
properties of matter. So, in the same way, consciousness is often referred to, so far as the reality is concerned,
as facts of the same order as physical processes; that
is, as "phenomena" and "symbols of the unknown."
Thus, to requote Mr. Spencer: "When with these
conclusions, that matter and motion, as we think them,
are but symbols of unknowable forms of existence, we
join the conclusion lately reached, that mind also is unknowable, and that the simplest form under which we
can think of its substance is but a *symbol of something*
that can never be rendered into thought, we see that
the whole question is at least nothing more than the
question whether these symbols should be expressed in
terms of those, or those in terms of these,—a question

scarcely worth deciding, since either answer leaves us as completely outside of the reality as we were at first." [1]

Now it may very properly be questioned whether a state of mind, as a *feeling*, can be conceived of as a *symbol* of its own substance. We can say an idea of anything external to us, as of a tree, is only a symbol of the actual something which exists there; for the *idea* of a tree is only the *effect* which the *actual* object produces on the mind, just as the impression in wax of a seal is a representation or symbol of the seal; or better, as the printed word is a symbol of the idea it represents, but, as a printed form, has nothing in common with that idea.

But in this case there are required and present two things,—one, the something to be symbolized, the tree-in-itself, and the other, the something in which the symbol is to be formed, the mind, and one is distinct from the other. But for a state of mind to be a *symbol* of its own substance, it is requisite that this particular state of mind should have an existence separate from that underlying substance, or, in other words, separate from itself. Otherwise the state of mind could not be acted upon by the substance. But if it is separate, it is a distinct entity, and then this underlying something cannot be the substance of mind. In brief, to quote Mr. Spencer himself in another connection, " A thing cannot at the same instant be both subject and object of thought, and yet the substance of mind must be this before it" can be both the symbol and the thing symbolized.

Whatever view be taken regarding the existence and

---

[1] Op. cit., p. 159.

nature of a something underlying consciousness, it is quite evident that the latter cannot be regarded as facts of the same order as its "accompanying" physical changes, as is done when both are regarded as symbols of something else.

This same looseness of thought and language has led to physical and mental processes being regarded as different "*aspects*" of the same thing.

Even so acute a thinker as Mr. Lewes has described mind and physical changes as different "aspects of one and the same process." This cannot be the correct conception, for it also makes matter and feeling facts of the same order. If mind and matter are to be regarded as "aspects," it must be that either they are aspects of each other or of a third thing, as of Spencer's substance of mind.

In the former case matter might be regarded as an aspect of mind, but mind cannot be imagined as an aspect of matter, as appears to be meant when Lewes says, "a mental process is only another aspect of a physical process."[1] Now a physical process may certainly be looked upon as an aspect of· a mental process, because it is the *effect* of the mental process on another organism, but the mental process being the actuality of the physical process,—the physical process in itself,— there is nothing for it to be an effect or aspect of. What has been said in regard to the conception of mind as a symbol is equally applicable here.

Under the second alternative, that they are different aspects of an underlying substance, physical processes may also be aspects, but mental processes not. For,

---

[1] Physical Basis of Mind, p. 386.

in order that the latter may be an aspect of this substance, there must be another substance or mind on which the underlying substance can work to produce the effect or aspect called consciousness. But where is there such another substance? We each of us have only one mind apiece.

This may be expressed in another way. To speak of anything as an aspect of something else implies something perceived and something perceiving, and the effect of the former upon the latter is the aspect of the former, the thing perceived. Now for consciousness to be an aspect of the substance of mind there is required, in addition to this substance, another thing or mind to perceive it, and consciousness must be the effect of the former upon the latter. But where is this second mind? There is none. Such an assumption would require a second entity, as a spirit. Therefore, if matter is an aspect, or the reaction of an organism to something else, consciousness cannot be aspect. The two can never be spoken of as facts of the same class. Besides, as was said in Chapter I., if these two classes of facts could be regarded as simply the subjective and objective aspects of one and the same thing, it would fall far short of offering us an adequate explanation, and would involve us in many difficulties such as have been pointed out.

Exception may be taken to that meaning of the term "aspect" which I have employed. But if aspect is not to be taken in its ordinary and exact sense, then it must mean very little or anything that one may choose, and is still more objectionable as an interpretation of the question.

The same objection holds to the expression that matter and mind are only "different modes of apprehending the same thing." Consciousness cannot be a mode of apprehending something else, because this also implies the existence of something else that apprehends. What is it?

Again, if by the term matter be meant the conscious states by which things-in-themselves are known to us, then matter and mind are plainly not two different aspects of the same fact. On the contrary, they are clearly *different psychical facts.* The sensation of mental tremors is one fact, the conscious state which is the reality of those tremors is another fact. Each is a subjective fact occurring in separate organisms. The conscious state called a sensation of color takes place in organism A, for example, and the conscious state called neural tremors in organism B, which is observing A. But the conscious state in A is the cause of the conscious state in B, which latter can, in this sense only, be said to be an aspect of the state of A, but not *vice versa.*

If by matter be meant not phenomena, but the thing-in-itself, then still less can matter and mind be regarded as different aspects of the same fact. For by cerebral tremors we now mean the reality of these tremors, and, as I have endeavored to demonstrate, this reality and consciousness are one and the same fact. This will become intelligible if the reader will refer to what was said regarding the meaning of the term matter in Chapter II.

On pursuing this mode of inquiry further, certain important results follow, which it will be necessary for us to consider.

Let us suppose a complicated apparatus, as of microscopes, by which B observes what takes place in A's brain when he has a sensation of color, for example; and C observes what occurs in B's brain at the same instant. Then it would happen that at the moment when A has the sensation of redness, B has the sensation of cerebral tremors, and also C has a sensation of tremors. This may be graphically represented as follows:

We have then the following as a result of these conditions:

In organism A : Sensation of color ; an actuality and the reality of,

In organism B : Cerebral tremors ; a conscious state, and as such also a reality, but also commonly known as phenomena or matter when projected outside of the organism and given objective existence in A. It is the form in which color in A is symbolized in B.

In organism C : Cerebral tremors ; a conscious state, and as such an actuality, and the form in which the conscious state in B is symbolized in C.

Cerebral tremors, then, are a conscious state, which may be a form of apprehending in a second organism either,

*f*

1st. An unlike conscious state,—sound, color, thought, etc.

2d. A similar conscious state or cerebral tremor.

In this instance of C, then, we are brought to what seems at first the surprising fact, that that conscious state called cerebral tremors, which is the cognition of the thing-in-itself, and known as phenomena, and the thing-in-itself, also cerebral tremors in B, are similar though separate facts. And under the conditions just mentioned it might almost be said that neural tremors exist outside of us as such; or in other words, *that such phenomena exist practically as we see them.* I say practically, for although the conscious state, neural motions, possessed by one organism, may be perceived by another also as neural motions in the brain of the former, still it does not follow that these first motions would be perceived as the same kind of motion. They would be perceived as motion of some kind, but not necessarily as the same kind. For instance, taking the same illustration used above, A's sensation of color might be perceived by B as undulatory motion; the conscious state of undulatory motion in B might be perceived as circular motion by C; which again might be represented in D's consciousness by spiral motion, and so on. I do not mean to say that these particular motions do actually exist. That would depend upon physical conditions not yet understood. All I mean is that some kind of motion or physical change may under some conditions be the mode of apprehending a motion which may or may not be the same in kind; and we perceive the thing-in-itself as it really exists.

# CHAPTER V.

## THE CORRELATION OF FORCES.

WE have now arrived at a position to consider another element in this problem, and one for which it is essential to find a satisfactory explanation. I refer to the law of the Correlation of Forces. If states of mind are simply states of matter, it is insisted they must be brought into harmony with all those general laws which govern the phenomena of matter. The difficulty of finding an application of this law to mental conditions has been generally recognized, and this difficulty has been taken advantage of by those styling themselves "anti-materialists," and urged with considerable force as an objection. Unless this objection can be met, materialism must admit a vulnerable point. For those who are unfamiliar with physical science, it will be necessary for a thorough comprehension of the argument to state with some fulness the meaning and application of the phrase "correlation of forces." I cannot do this better than in the words of Mr. Fiske, who at the same time forcibly states the objections we are obliged to meet: "Let us now apply these principles to the case of an organism, such as the human body. All of the 'force'—i.e., capacity of motion—present at any moment in the human body is derived from the food that we eat and the air that we breathe. As food is

turned into oxygenated blood and assimilated with
the various tissues of the body, which themselves represent previously assimilated food, the molecular movements of the food material become variously combined
into molecular movements in tissue,—in muscular tissue,
in adipose, in cellular, and in nerve tissue, and so on.
Every undulation that takes place among the molecules
of a nerve represents some simpler form of molecular
motion contained in food that has been assimilated ;
and for every given quantity of the former kind of
motion that appears, an equivalent quantity of the
latter kind disappears in producing it.   And so we may
go on, keeping the account strictly balanced, until we
reach the peculiar discharge of undulatory motion between cerebral ganglia that uniformly accompanies a
feeling or state of consciousness.   What now occurs?
*Along with this peculiar undulatory motion there occurs
a feeling,—the primary element of a thought or of an
emotion.*   But does the motion *produce*[1] the feeling
in the same sense that heat produces light?   *Does a
given quantity of motion disappear, to be replaced by an
equivalent quantity of feeling ?*   By no means.   The
nerve-motion in disappearing is simply distributed into
other nerve-motions in various parts of the body, and then
other nerve-motions, in their turn, become variously
metamorphosed into motions of contraction in muscles,
motions of secretion in glands, motions of assimilation
in tissues generally, or into yet other nerve-motions.
Nowhere is there such a thing as the metamorphosis
of motion into feeling, or of feeling into motion.   Of

---

[1] Italics in the original, but the other italics are mine.

course I do not mean that the circuit, as thus described, has ever been experimentally traced, or that it can be experimentally traced. What I mean is, that if the law of the ' correlation of forces' is to be applied at all to the physical processes which go on within the living organism, we are of necessity bound to render our whole account into terms of motion that can be quantitatively measured. Once admit into the circuit some element —such as feeling—that does not allow of quantitative measurement, and the correlation can no longer be established; we are landed at once into absurdity and contradiction. So far as the correlation of forces has anything to do with it, the entire circle of transmutation, from the lowest physico-chemical motion all the way up to the highest nerve-motion and all the way down again to the lowest physico-chemical motion, must be described in physical terms, and no account whatever can be taken of any such thing as feeling or consciousness." [1]

The reader will immediately perceive how the idea of feeling, being something more than and in addition to those activities called motion, pervades the whole passage. This is especially evident in those passages indicated by italics. " *Along with this peculiar undulatory motion there occurs a feeling,—the primary element of a thought or of an emotion.*" " *Does a given quantity of motion disappear, to be replaced by an equivalent quantity of feeling ?*" The idea of feeling being something plus physical activities could hardly be more plainly stated. With this false conception as a

[1] North Am. Rev., loc. cit.

starting-point, the conclusion affirming the inapplicability of the correlation of forces naturally follows.

After what has been said in the preceding chapters, the reader will, without difficulty, recognize the fallacy of this conception of double processes, no matter whether the second property be looked upon as spiritual or physical. It leads, as was averred on page 25, and as Mr. Fiske has well shown, to the destruction of the universality of this law of correlation. But materialism must not be blamed for the shortcomings of its interpreters or the misconceptions of its opponents. If it can be shown that materialism cannot be reconciled with the law of the correlation of forces, materialism must fall. But this is far from being the case. When Materialism is properly understood no such difficulty is met with. Before consigning any doctrine to oblivion, it would be becoming in its opponents to examine once more their own interpretation of that doctrine, and see if the fault does not lie with themselves. Having begun by misunderstanding the doctrine of materialism, they naturally end by finding fault with errors which are of their own making. They should be more careful not to mistake their own blunders for those of nature.

But is this statement just quoted respecting the inapplicability of the law of the Correlation of Forces to Mind true of that interpretation of materialism maintained in these pages? Let us see. "Along with this peculiar form of undulatory motion there occurs a feeling,—the primary element of a thought or of an emotion." This is not correct. There are not two things which occur simultaneously in one organism.

There occurs solely the Feeling, and the undulatory motion is only the subjective expression of another person's perception of this feeling. Therefore it obviously cannot be said that the motion *produces* the feeling, for the two are one.

"Does a given quantity of motion disappear, to be replaced by an equivalent quantity of feeling?" If the term "motion" is here employed to represent that cerebral motion which is commonly though incorrectly said to accompany a feeling, the answer must be "No," for the reason just given. But if it is used to designate those motions which occur in the sensory nerves, and *if we bear in mind what we mean by such motion,* an affirmative answer may be given. Let me explain by an illustration what I mean. Let us suppose that we have been pricked in the arm by a pin. As a result we have a sensation of pain, which in turn causes us to withdraw the arm. We have here what is called a nervous circuit. In the sensory nerve going to the brain there is excited some "nerve-motion," which in turn travels to the cerebral centres, where this motion is exchanged for cerebral motion in the cells of the brain. From hence it issues again along the motor nerves as nerve-motion, until it finally reaches the muscles to become muscular motion. Here is a dynamic circuit. But where is *feeling?* Has it entered into it? Not at all; because we have been employing physical terms. We cannot change one term of the equation without changing all the others to correspond, any more than we can add quarts and pounds together, but each must be reduced to the same standard of measurement. If we wish to bring feeling into the circuit, we must employ a corresponding set of symbols. It will then be expressed as follows: The molecular disturbances in the nerves, designated by nerve-motion, must be represented by the term " unknown $x$." The difficulty is that the ordinary use of language carries with it pitfalls and dangers, which can only be avoided by keeping constantly before the mind the reality which is represented by the word. When we talk of nerve-motions, the most wary are liable to be misled; and even the more general term "physical disturbance or activity" contains an idea of something that we see or feel, and the unknown conditions for which it stands are lost sight of. In this way terms of different measurement are introduced into the equation, and the real question becomes lost in one of words.

It is better, when dealing with *ultimates*, as we are when we talk of feeling, to employ such indefinite terms as $x$ or $y$, which have no preconceived notions attached to them, instead of speaking of motions and undulations which are not ultimates. Letting $x$, then, stand for the unknown changes in the sensory nerves, and $y$ for those in the motor, we can say that *unknown x* becomes transformed into an equivalent amount of consciousness; that consciousness becomes again transformed into an equivalent amount of *unknown y*, and with each metamorphosis a certain amount of the one factor disappears, to be replaced by an equivalent amount of the succeeding factor. We have here, then, a circuit of ultimates corresponding to and identical with the dynamic nervous circuit, and the principle of " correlation of forces" becomes applicable to the facts of consciousness.

But is it necessary that we should use these indefinite expressions in order that this law of correlation
may be applied to the subjective world? I think not, if,
as I have said so many times before, we are careful not
to mistake the symbol for the reality symbolized. We
can say that in traversing the nervous circuit the nerve-
motion in the sensory nerves becomes transformed into
an equivalent amount of cerebral motion, or consciousness, which in turn disappears to become nerve-motion
again. But now we must remember that "cerebral
motion" and consciousness are one and the same thing.
Only the former is a symbol of the latter. Not
the gold and silver side of an iron shield, but a gold
shield, one side of which has been silvered. If we
wish to measure these motions by mechanical apparatus,
of course it must be the cerebral motions, not consciousness, which are to be measured; for mechanical methods
can only be applied to the conditions to meet which
they were designed. I have discussed the application
of this law of the correlation of forces in a very general way, referring only to the principles underlying it.
It would take us too far out of our way to consider all
the complex conditions entering into the equation of
its application,—what amount of "nerve-motion," for
example, in a sensory nerve passes into other nerve-
motions in outgoing nerves without the intervention
of consciousness; how much becomes transformed into
consciousness; how much finds its equivalent in disturbances in the sympathetic system and in nutritive
tissue change; and, finally, how much consciousness
is balanced by the previous molecular action of the
food storing up, so to speak, mind-force in the cells of

the brain, ready to be discharged like a mine of gun-powder on lighting the fuse. These questions physiology is not sufficiently developed to answer at present.

If the distinctions dwelt upon above are borne in mind, the difficulty ceases to be one of mere words, and one of the strongest objections to the materialistic doctrine of mind is avoided. We see how movement may be the cause of thought, and thought of movement. The assertion of Lange,[1] that "were it possible for a single cerebral atom to be moved by 'thought' so much as the millionth of a millimetre out of the path due to it by the laws of mechanics, the whole 'formula of the universe' would become inapplicable and senseless," can only be maintained on the assumption that mind is something more than matter, a spiritual entity.

Thought can move an atom, for it can move the un-known ultimate which is the basis of that group of phenomena we call an atom. But to insist upon this precision of statement is a mere quibble over words, though the superficial criticisms of Lange[2] may sometimes render it necessary.

---

[1] History of Materialism.
[2] Ibid., vol. iii. p. 9.

# PART II.

## HUMAN AUTOMATISM.

"WHEREFORE, as men owe all their true ratiocination in the right understanding of speech, so also they owe their errors to the misunderstanding of the same; and as all the ornaments of philosophy proceed only from men, so from man also is derived the ugly absurdity of false opinions. For speech has something in it like to a spider's web (as it was said of old of Solon's laws), for by contexture of words tender and delicate wits are ensnared and stopped, but strong wits break easily through them."

HOBBES.

91

# CHAPTER I.

## THE REFLEX CHARACTER OF IDEAS.

HAVING thus far been occupied with the consideration of the nature of mind, we are now prepared to enter upon the second part of our subject, or Human Automatism. But as what will follow consists only of deductions from the principles laid down in the preceding chapters, it was absolutely essential that we should first see that these principles were well established and clearly understood. It is to be hoped that this has been done, and that that interpretation of materialism has been given which is both consistent with the facts and affords a complete explanation of the mystery of consciousness. It is because proper pains have not always been taken to establish the correctness of the first principles, that such extraordinary and indefensible deductions have sometimes been drawn.

We have seen how consciousness is nothing more than the reality of those physical processes we call undulations, and that the latter are only the means by which consciousness becomes known to us when apprehended by a second person through the senses,—in fact, the symbols of consciousness.

But this doctrine involves logical consequences from which there can be no escape, and which we cannot avoid considering.

As physical processes are symbols and equivalents of consciousness, we can, through the physical method, let them stand for mental processes, study them as such equivalents, and investigate the conditions under which they arise.    Afterwards we can translate the results into terms of consciousness.

Now that matter, of which consciousness is the reality, must be subject to the laws which govern matter. One of these laws is the law of inertia.    According to this, matter cannot of itself change its own state.    Matter at rest must forever remain at rest, unless something outside of itself disturbs it and puts it in motion. Matter in motion must forever persist in motion till something outside of it checks it.    Matter exhibited under one property must forever be exhibited under that property, unless some external force causes it to be exhibited under another.    Whatever be the state of matter at a given moment, it must always remain in that state till outside agencies effect a change.    This is a universal law; it has no exception.    To this law, then, the "matter of the mind" must be subject.    Let us apply it and see what it means.    It means this: that no change of any kind, chemical or physical, can occur in the protoplasm of the brain without the interference of outside agencies; that no vibration or pulsation can occur among the protoplasmic molecules of any cell unless some cause external to that cell acts upon them; that for the undulations of the molecules—of which consciousness is the reality—to occur, some external force is requisite to start them into activity; in other words, for consciousness to be present it is necessary that each cell should be stimulated by something exter-

nal to that cell.[1]　The activity of the molecules of no
cell can appear spontaneously, and hence neither can
the reality of that activity, or consciousness. *Consciousness, then, is passive, not active;* it is conditioned existence, not unconditioned; it is a link in a series of
events.

Such is the inevitable result to which our reasoning
leads us. If consciousness depends on matter being
disturbed, it must be passive. This is a logical consequence of our premises, from which there is no escape.
But if our thoughts are passive,—if they are merely
the molecular disturbances in themselves and cannot
arise spontaneously,—it must be that the stimulus required for their production cannot be applied in any
indefinite manner at haphazard, but only through the
anatomical mechanism of the brain,—only through the
nerve-conductors developed for the purpose. The
channels by which stimuli from without reach the cells
of the brain are the centripetal nerves; and any succession
of ideas can only occur by reason of the neural "cur-

---

[1] Objection may be made to this on the ground that, consciousness being the reality, the laws which govern phenomena cannot
be applied to it. But I have already shown (Chapter V.) that by
a change of all the terms in the series the law of correlation of
forces may be extended to mental processes. Furthermore, the
physical process being the equivalent and symbol of the mental
process, we can substitute the one for the other; and having
worked out the problem, retranslate the results back again into
the original terms. It is not possible to conceive of the neural
vibrations being absent or present without its reality, consciousness, being similarly absent or present; and anything which,
from a physical point of view, causes the occurrence of the
vibrations must, from a psychological point of view, have an
equivalent result in consciousness.

rents," wherever originated, being reflected from one
cell to another along the anatomical connections which
join the cells ; and any objective expression of an idea
can only take place by reason of the current passing
again from the brain to the organs of expression, which
are the muscles.    In other words, under normal conditions, *every muscular action, every idea, sensation, or
emotion requires for its production some stimulus originating outside of its own nervous centre,—that is, it is
reflex.*[1]

I think it is possible to show, by reference to the
facts of physiology and pathology, that from the simplest muscular act, such as the winking of the eyelid,
to the most complex muscular actions and trains of
thought, there is never a difference in kind, only one of
degree; that we can pass from one to the other by a
series of gradations, step by step, and find them all of
the same nature, reflex in character.

There is one objection to this conclusion respecting
the reflex character of ideas which, at first sight, appears plausible, but yet, whatever validity it may have,
does essentially affect the principle of the hypothesis.
It may be urged (and, from a philosophical point of
view, correctly) that, even if the physical process in the
brain be a reflex one, this term, which derives its meaning from physical conditions, cannot be applied to de-

---

[1] There is one probable exception to this, and that is when
ideas under abnormal conditions are caused by direct irritation of
the blood, as in delirium, or by foreign substances, as opium.   But
in this case the ideas are still passive, and it is probable that only
some of these ideas are due to direct irritation and the remainder
are reflected, as shown by the association of allied ideas.

note the character of psychical facts. When we say, for
instance, that certain nervous processes are reflex, we
mean that the neural current passes along certain ingoing nerves to certain groups of neural cells in the
brain; that then the current, after having started certain reactions in the molecules of the cells, is reflected
from cell to cell, a similar effect being produced in each;
and, finally, that the current is reflected outwards along
certain outgoing paths to the muscles, to end in action
of some kind. We can even form a picture in the
mind of all this, and perhaps graphically represent it
on paper. But no such picture can be drawn to illus-
trate the relation of the psychical facts, the ideas, which
are the reality and correspond to this process. We
can see that one idea is invariably associated with another idea; that one follows another according to certain laws of thought, which we can formulate from our
former experience. But this association is nothing like
the picture we formed of the reflex physical process.
All this is undoubtedly true, but nevertheless it cannot
be regarded as a fatal objection to the hypothesis advanced, nor as irreconcilable with all the facts. Ideas
are the reality of the physical process, and though they
cannot, by a strict use of terms, be said to be reflex,
still the relations between them are of a nature that
*correspond* to the reflex physical process; so that ideas
in some way, which possibly cannot be translated into
thought, are bound together in a fashion which has its
counterpart in the reflected neural current and cellular
commotions. The reality of the cellular commotions
are ideas, and the reflected physical process is the manner in which these realities are recognized by us when

apprehended through the senses.  This use of physical terms to describe subjective conditions need not be fallacious or regarded as unphilosophical if we only have in mind the conditions for which the terms stand.[1]

---

[1] See also note to page 96.

# CHAPTER II.

## CONSCIOUSNESS AS AN AGENT IN THE DETERMI-
## NATION OF BODILY ACTION.

THE outcome of our inquiry thus far has resulted in a theory which both explains the "relationship of the mind to the body," and also the mechanism by which mental action takes place. This theory at once satisfies all the conditions of the case, and explains the mysteries which have so long hung about the problem. We have seen how the very question, "How is the mind related to matter?" involves erroneous assumptions regarding the nature of each, which make the question itself an absurd one. In the reflex theory of ideas we find a mechanism by which the human mind carries on all its manifold operations, from the simplest mental act, like the sudden start of the body at the sound of a cannon, to the most complex train of thought. In passing from the more simple to the more complex the paths of thought become more circuitous and more complicated, but the process does not change. The difference is in degree, not in kind. On the physical side the current is reflected from cell to cell till it finally ends in the outgoing current which terminates in muscular action; and on the mental side, each thought, which is the reality of the physical process, is attached, so to speak, in some unknown way to each succeeding thought in such a manner that one necessa-

99

rily ensues upon the other, according to certain psychological laws.    Every idea calls up the particular idea
which is associated with it in the same chain of ideas,
to end finally, also, in muscular action ; though, as each
chain is linked with hundreds of other chains which
cross its paths, fresh stimuli may switch the current of
ideas along these connecting chains into fresh circuits.

To this reflex view there are logical consequences from
which I see no escape.    From the theory that a mental
process is the reality of the reflex physiological process
to the doctrine of automatism is a step which we are
compelled by the force of logical necessity to take, or
rather, the two doctrines are essentially the same.    For
any doctrine which removes our thoughts from the
control of a hypothetical agent which is independent
of external influences, and confines them to certain
channels in which they are propelled, directly or indirectly, by stimuli (external or internal) is practically
automatism.    Under the reflex view, spontaneity, in the
sense that any idea or state of mind can arise except as
the resultant of some other idea by which it is conditioned, is impossible.    Reflex is, consequently, equivalent to automatic.

On the other hand, the automatism which we are
compelled to adopt is modified in a most important
particular by the discovery of the relation which mind
bears to matter.    By this modification the principal
objection to automatism is removed.    As we have
already seen (Chapter I.), and as we shall presently see
more fully, some automatists, from a failure to take into
account the testimony of direct consciousness, have
given expression to a theory according to which all

our actions are accomplished by the physiological mechanism of the brain, without being influenced in any way by volition or feeling. These latter are limited to the part of indicators to tell how the physical machinery beneath is working, nothing more. Any such notion of automatism can only arise from an ill-digested consideration of the facts and a total misconception of the problem in question. Now, on the contrary, the form of automatism which is the outcome of the reflex theory we have formed takes into account the testimony offered directly by consciousness, and recognizes fully the part played by volition in acting on the bodily mechanism and determining our actions. The great merit of the doctrine of the nature of mind which has been adopted in these pages is that it harmonizes our subjective and objective knowledge, and not only allows to consciousness the power of acting on the molecules of matter, but renders intelligible *how* it acts. Consciousness is as much an agent in determining physical action as molecular motion is,— nay, it is more.

That I do this or that because I *feel* so and so is a psychological fact beyond dispute. No amount of reasoning can argue me out of the belief that I drink this water because I am thirsty. But this is only stating the problem in other terms,—in psychological instead of physiological terms,—and does not in any way contradict our hypothesis. We can indifferently say that any action is dependent upon the organic connection of the nervous elements, or say it is dependent upon our feelings. It must be remembered that a subjective process and a neural disturbance are, at bottom, one and the same thing, and either may be said to be the cause of the ensuing action, if we bear in mind the terms in which the fact is expressed. But in one sense it is more correct to speak in terms of feeling and thought than in those of matter. Ideas, sensations, etc., are the ultimates, the final terms to which phenomena can be reduced. They are actualities, and well known to us, while physical undulations, etc., are not, being merely phenomena. Hence it is more correct to use psychological terms, in speaking of mental "phenomena," than physical terms.

It was shown in a preceding chapter how, from a misunderstanding of the real relation between mind and physical changes,—how, from the conception of consciousness being something in addition to neural undulations,—the conclusion naturally follows that, as muscular action was only in direct connection with the physical changes of the brain, consciousness, which was something more and outside the former, could have nothing to do with the production of our actions, and must be merely a collateral product. This conclusion followed logically from the premises, but was also drawn unwarrantably from certain experiments on animals. The bearing of these experiments upon the point at issue will be discussed presently. We are now considering this conclusion as a logical deduction from the premises referred to. The adversaries of the modern doctrine, as well as its disciples, were not slow to point out that it is a psychological *fact* that our feelings are the cause of our actions,—that when we rub a spot where we have been bitten by a mosquito, we do it *because* we *feel* uncomfortably at that spot. This is a fact which every one can verify as often as he pleases. This being so, the logical inference which should be drawn is that there is some fallacy in the premises. But the opponents went further, and inferred that if our feelings are the cause of our actions, then we cannot be automata. This is an unjustifiable inference because there is no evidence that one excludes the other. It has been thought that we could only be automata on the supposition that our feelings were collateral products. Now, on the contrary, I maintain; first, that our feelings are *not* collateral products; second, that they are the active agents; and, third, that nevertheless we are automata.

This conception that feeling as agent necessarily excludes automatism is expressed by G. H. Lewes in the following paragraph :

" The question of automatism, which has been argued in the preceding chapters, may, I think, be summarily disposed of by a reference to the irresistible evidence each man carries in his own consciousness that his actions are frequently, even if not always, determined by feelings. He is quite certain that he is not an automaton, and that his feelings are not simply collateral products of his actions, without the power of modifying and originating them."

Now in this passage there is really contained a syllogism which may be expressed as follows :

" If Feeling determines action, and is not a collateral product, we are not automata. Consciousness proves that Feeling does determine action; ergo, we are not automata."

Now the point maintained here is, that the first

premise is incorrect; hence the conclusion is invalid. Feeling may be the cause of physical action, and the whole be still automatic.

If our hypothesis regarding the nature of the mind be the correct one, and feeling and physical changes be practically the same thing, it follows that one is as much the cause of physical actions as the other, and one is as automatic as the other.

It is proper to state that these are not the main reasons which Mr. Lewes gives for rejecting the theory of automatism. On the contrary, a large portion of his work is devoted to an elaborate exposition of his views on this question. It would carry us too far out of the way to enter into an examination of them, involving as they do questions which are far beyond the limits set for this work. Suffice it to say that Mr. Lewes devotes considerable space to a discussion of the functions of automata, and to the question whether unconscious and reflex actions are governed by Sensibility. Finding that automata have not Sensibility, and also holding that all our actions, those that are conscious and unconscious, as well as those ordinarily called reflex, are governed by Sensibility, he concludes that the human organism is not an automaton. We cannot enter into the question as to how far sensibility enters into so-called unconscious actions, as it is not essential to our argument. From our point of view it makes no difference whether the so-called unconscious actions are guided by Sensibility or not; in either case our answer would be the same. I am ready, however, to follow Mr. Lewes some distance, and allow sensibility to many "unconscious" actions.

As, for instance, when walking through the crowded streets we avoid the passers-by though our thoughts are deeply intent on something else. We certainly have the optical sensations of the passing crowd, and are guided by them, though at the time we are unconscious of the sensations. On the other hand, there are many reflex actions to which no subjective quality can be attached, and which cannot be governed by anything of the nature of sensibility, unless by sensibility is merely meant a neural reaction as opposed to other physical reactions, in which case the question becomes one only of terms.

Even if conscious and unconscious actions be governed by Sensibility, they may still be automatic. To be sure, a sentient action is not in one sense of the term a mechanical one, for no mechanical toy has consciousness or sensibility of any kind. If it be maintained that nothing is automatic which has consciousness and is worked by sensations, then we are not on this definition automata. But this limitation of the word automatism is not in my opinion essential.

When it is said that mental processes are automatic, I do not conceive that it is necessarily meant that we are identical with or like machines in every particular. For instance, human beings grow and generate other human beings, functions not possessed by machines. When it is said that we are automata, or that our mental processes are automatic, I understand that all that is meant is that our thoughts, sensations, volitions, and actions follow in certain grooves or channels which have their analogies and equivalents in the anatomical mechanism of the brain, and that the presence of every

state of mind is conditioned by the anatomical structure and physiological working of the brain. Automatism is then synonymous with reflex action.[1] The
theory of automatism is antithetical to the spiritual
doctrine which postulates a central unconditioned Ego
holding undisputed sway over our actions.

" But," says Mr. Lewes, " it [organized experience]
cannot be made to enter into the mechanism of an automaton, because, however complex that mechanism
may be, and however capable of variety of action, it
is constructed solely for definite actions on calculated
lines; all its readjustments must have been foreseen,
it is incapable of adjusting itself to unforeseen circumstances. Hence every interruption in the prearranged
order either throws it out of gear, or brings it to a
standstill. It is regulated, not self-regulating. The
organism, on the contrary,—conspicuously so in its more
complex forms,—is variable, self-regulating, incalcu-
lable. It has *selective adaptation* responding readily
and efficiently to novel and unforeseen circumstances,
acquiring new modes of combination and reaction.
An automaton that will learn by experience, and adapt
itself to conditions not calculated for in its construction,
has yet to be made; till it is made we must deny that
organisms are machines."[2] Using the same method of
reasoning we may answer, such a machine has been
made, not by man, it is true, but by nature. In the
human organism we find such an automaton made by
natural forces.

---

[1] Mr. Lewes admits that all mental action is reflex.
[2] Physical Basis of Mind, p. 433.

The part which feeling plays in our action is a point of great importance, and it seems to me that it is from a failure to thoroughly grasp it that many materialists have been led into error and have laid themselves open to criticism. And, if I am right, even such an acute thinker as Professor Huxley seems to have become involved in this fallacy. "The consciousness of brutes," he says, "would appear to be related to the mechanism of their body simply as a collateral product of its working, and to be as completely without the power of modifying that working as the steam whistle, which accompanies the work of a locomotive engine, is without influence upon its machinery." Their volition, if they have any, is an emotion indicative of physical changes, not a cause of such changes.[1]

Again, "It seems to me that in men as in brutes there is no proof that any state of consciousness is the cause of change in the motion of matter of the organism. If these positions are well based, it follows that our mutual conditions are simply the symbols in consciousness of the changes which take place automatically in the organism : and that to take an extreme illustration, the feeling we call volition is not the cause of a voluntary act, but the symbol of that state of the brain which is the immediate cause of that act."[2]

I must be pardoned if I dissent from so distinguished a writer. I cannot agree with the statement "that consciousness is related to the mechanical working of the body simply as a collateral product of its working ;" nor can I admit the slightest analogy between it and

---

[1] Fortnightly Review, November, 1874.    [2] Ibid.

the steam whistle of a locomotive.  It seems to me, if
the theory of consciousness which has been adopted in
these pages be the correct one, that consciousness has
the greatest power of modifying the working of the
body.    That I rub my arm because I have pain there,
and because I have in my mind an idea that I shall
relieve that pain if I rub it, seems to me to be an
incontrovertible fact.    You may employ the physiological method, if you please, and by using an artifice
state the fact in physical terms instead of psychological.
You may then say that the muscular action requisite
for the act of rubbing is the consequence of molecular
disturbances in the brain.    This is absolutely true.
But these so-called molecular disturbances are *in reality*
consciousness, and hence consciousness is just as much
the cause of the "working of the body" as these molecular disturbances.    Any other conception than this
involves a paradox.

I am unable to quite understand how it can be said
that " our mental conditions are simply the symbols in
consciousness of the changes which take place automatically in the organism," if that idea of the nature of
consciousness which I have endeavored to make intelligible in the preceding pages is clearly borne in mind.

There are only two hypotheses respecting the nature
of consciousness which are compatible with this notion
of its being a "collateral product," and neither of these
can be logically established.    First, it may be supposed
that consciousness is a distinct entity existing beyond
the physiological changes in the brain.    That when an
idea is present, there are brought into existence two
things,—that which we call a physical change plus

something more, an idea, and this idea is something produced or secreted. I have already shown that this is impossible; that if it were the case this idea, the second entity, must be either material or *immaterial,* neither of which conditions are within the bounds of probabilities. If my reasoning be not false, consciousness is nothing more than the *reality* of these physical changes. When the brain is irritated we have feeling as a result, while physical changes are only the mode by which another person ideally perceives it.

The second hypothesis offers the most legitimate interpretation of the doctrine we are considering, and it is the one which I believe is in harmony with Professor Huxley's views. I do not wish to misrepresent him, but I am unable to discover in his expressed opinions any other meaning which is logically compatible with the view of "our mental conditions being only symbols in consciousness," etc.

According to this second hypothesis feeling is a "property" or "function of matter," but it must be a second function which has an existence in addition to and parallel with that function we call physical change. Whenever physical change occurs, then the function of consciousness appears side by side with it. This view has already been discussed in Chapter I., and reasons given to show its want of validity. It has been shown that there is nothing in the second function which cannot be as well explained through the first (physical change); it is not applicable to the law of the correlation of forces; it leads to the denial of feeling being an active agent in the production of our actions. Any such conclusion as this last must be an absurdity on the

10

face of it. The objections urged by Dr. Carpenter and Mr. Martineau [1] are well founded, namely, that it renders consciousness superfluous, and it would necessarily follow that all our acts and doings, both mental and physical, the greatest works of poets, the paintings of artists, and the labors of statesmen could be as well performed without consciousness as with it. This reduces such a conception to a paradox and absurdity.

This opinion, to which Professor Huxley has given expression, was apparently based on some well-known experiments on animals, and soon aroused considerable opposition and discussion. It has not appeared that the results of these experiments would warrant any such inference being drawn from them. But as whatever is said or written by this distinguished scientist has necessarily very great weight, and as these expressions in particular attracted much attention, I do not think it will be considered superfluous to take the time to consider the bearing which these experiments above referred to have on the question at issue. They, together with the phenomena of hypnotism, somnambulism, and kindred states, have thrown more light on the problems of consciousness than all other discoveries in nervous physiology.

A frog, *from which the cerebral hemispheres have been removed*, that is to say, that portion of the brain which is concerned with intelligence, volition, and the other higher faculties, is still capable of executing all the movements natural to it, *under certain conditions.* If such a frog, for example, be placed on the palm of the hand, and the

---

[1] Modern Materialism, by Rev. James Martineau.

hand then gently turned, the frog w ll crawl upwards
on the palm till it reaches the edge, and then as the
hand is still turned, it will crawl over upon the back
of the hand, when this becomes uppermost, where it
will remain quietly at rest if the hand is held in
this horizontal position. If the hand be again slowly
turned back to its original position, the frog will reverse
the process till it reaches the palm where it was first
placed. If again the frog be thrown into the water, it
will swim like a natural frog, but will keep on swimming until exhausted or till it strikes an obstacle, when
it will stop. If it strikes a board, it will crawl out
of the water on to it. If the creature be pinched, it
will hop, and if something be placed in its path, it will
jump one side out of the way and avoid it. If its
flanks be stroked, it will croak once for each stroke.
This it will do as regularly and without fail as an engine will whistle when you pull the steam-valve. But
if the creature be left alone, it will remain quiet for an
indefinite period and make no effort to eat or move.
All *desire* to do anything is lost. Whatever it does is
done only after having been prodded.

Similar experiments have been made on other animals, on pigeons, fishes, rats, etc., and with similar
results. A pigeon from which the cerebral hemispheres (including even the corpora striata and optic
thalami, two important centres at the base of the brain)
have been removed, is able still to stand on one leg
like an unmutilated bird which has gone to sleep. If
left alone, it remains quiet like a dull and sleepy bird.
If disturbed, it shifts its position. It dresses its
feathers and tucks its head under its wing. If food

be placed before it, it will not notice it, and will starve
if not artificially fed ; but if food be placed in its mouth,
it will swallow and chew like a natural bird.   If the
pigeon be thrown into the air it will fly, and its flight
can scarcely be distinguished from that of a normal
bird.   It will fly for a considerable distance and avoid
obstacles.   A fish thrown into the water swims like a
natural fish, and avoids obstacles with considerable
precision.   The rabbit and rat which have been similarly mutilated run and leap.   A pigeon was observed
by Flourens, who was first to experiment in this manner, to open its eyes on a pistol being fired off, " stretch
its neck, raise its head, and then fall back into its former
torpid attitude," but it showed no signs of fear.   It
sometimes followed the movements of the candle in
front of it.   Vulpian severed all connection between
the brain and spinal cord just above the medulla oblon-
gata in a rat; on pinching the foot the animal uttered
a sharp cry of pain.   "In another experiment he removed the cerebral hemispheres, the corpora striata,
and the optic thalami of the rat, when it remained
perfectly quiet; but immediately a sound of spitting
was made in imitation of that which a cat makes
sometimes, it made a bound away and repeated the
jump each time that the noise was made."

The actions of animals from which the brain has
been removed have been thus summarized by Onimus.

"As a summary, in the inferior animals, as in the
superior animals, the removal of the cerebral hemispheres does not cause to disappear any of the movements that previously existed, only these movements
assume certain peculiar characters.   In the first place,

they are more regular, they have the true normal type, for no psychical influence intervenes to modify them ; the locomotive apparatus is brought into action without interferences, and one could almost say that the *ensemble* of movements is the more normal than in the normal condition.

"In the second place, the movements executed take place inevitably after certain excitations. *It is a necessity* that the frog placed in water should swim, and that the pigeon thrown into the air should fly. The physiologist can then, at will, in an animal without the brain, determine such and such an act, limit it, arrest it ; he can anticipate the movements and affirm in advance that they will take place under certain conditions, absolutely as the chemist knows in advance the reactions that he will obtain in mixing certain bodies.

"Another peculiarity in the movements that take place, when the cerebral lobes are removed, is their continuation after a first impression. On the ground, a frog without the brain when irritated makes, in general, two or three jumps at the most ; it is rare that he makes but one. Placed in water, it continues the movement of natation until it meets with an obstacle ; it is the same in the carp, eel, etc. The pigeon continues to fly, the duck and goose continue to swim, etc. We should say that there is a spring which needs for its action a first impression, and which is stopped by the slightest resistance. But, what is striking, is precisely that continuation of the condition once determined, and we cannot refrain from connecting the facts observed in an animal deprived of the cerebral lobes with those which constitute the characteristic properties of inor-

h                     10*

ganic matter. Brought into movement, the animal without a brain retains the movement until there is exhaustion of the conditions of movement, or until it meets with resistance; taken in repose, it remains in the state of inertia until an exterior cause intervenes to bring it out of this condition. It is *living*, inert *matter.*" [1]

It is hardly necessary to enter into any extended discussion of these experiments. What they show is, that the movements habitual in the lower animals, as walking, running, flying, etc., as well as similar movements in man, are or may be performed without the continuous intervention of consciousness,[2] by a mechanism at the base of the brain. In the gray ganglia at the base is contained a clock-work which is capable of carrying on these movements when once the spring has been touched which sets it into action. The modes by which this spring may be touched are various. It may be directly through the sensory nerves without the intervention of the brain, as in the case of these experiments; in which case all movements will be performed without the influence of volition or consciousness: or it may be

---

[1] Flint's Physiology.

[2] To avoid misunderstanding, it should be stated that the term "consciousness" is used here in connection with these experiments to indicate that special mode of consciousness called self-consciousness, by which we are conscious of our sensations. It is not necessary for us to enter into the question whether these animals have any sensations or sensibility at all. What I am contending for is, that even granting they have no sensations or anything that can be imagined as a subjective state, that still they do not negative the conclusion that in the normal state consciousness, either in its general or special form, is a causative factor in our actions.

through the brain and intellect; in which case this clock-work will be directly under the control of volition. In the former case the response will naturally be machine-like after the cerebrum has been removed, for there will remain no force capable of modifying the reaction once begun; inasmuch as with the brain all volition and higher forms of consciousness have been destroyed. When the automatic mechanism has once begun to work, it will continue till either the clock has run down or a new stimulus to the sensory nerves has started a new reaction. But the movements which are carried on in this way are only those which are habitually performed by animals under normal conditions. The part which is normally played by that special form of consciousness called volition in all such movements, is to touch the spring and to regulate the workings of the mechanism, so as to adapt the latter to the changing wants of the organism.

While volition can interfere and direct each movement of the body, it habitually does so only when some new or unusual movement is to be performed, or some old combination of movement is to be adapted to altered conditions. We all know that even in man for such habitual movements as walking, speaking, writing, sewing, knitting, etc., consciousness of the muscular action employed is not necessary. We are accustomed to perform these actions mechanically, as we say, without being aware of each movement we make. Consciousness simply sets in motion the mechanism at the base of the brain. In this way a division of labor is effected. If we were obliged to keep our thoughts intent upon every movement we make, our brains would soon tire, and we would have little opportunity for thought and reflection upon the matter which the movements were intended to effect. If I were obliged to keep my mind intent upon the formation of each letter as I write, I should have little opportunity for thought concerning the matter about which I write.

In this important particular, then, the animal without a brain differs from the normal animal. Though all possible movements can be performed, they are not performed in the same manner as before. The animal has lost the faculty which in the normal condition modifies his movements; he has no intelligence or volition. He may be said to *know* nothing. The customary agency which guides him is gone. That agency is feeling. His past experience can serve him only so far as it has impressed itself in the mechanism at the base of the brain, and can become manifest only as a mechanical resultant to external impressions. Though all normal movements are performed, they are so only as necessary reactions to external stimuli, and in a stereotyped manner. While the animal reacts to a stimulus, it does not recognize what the stimulus is; it shows no fear or pleasure.

Though it is true that notwithstanding the loss of the brain, and also, therefore, of consciousness, the animal is capable of movements of a complicated character, *yet with this loss of consciousness there is also lost that very modification of the movements which is peculiar to the animal possessing consciousness, and which is effected by consciousness.* With the loss of consciousness there is lost also the especial manifestations of consciousness.

These experiments, then, plainly cannot be cited in evidence of the theory that volition has no influence in modifying bodily action. When properly examined they are capable of no such interpretations. On the contrary, they show that with the removal of the brain there is brought about just such a profound derangement of bodily functions as would be expected to follow from the withdrawal of consciousness; and the results harmonize completely with our knowledge of the functions of the brain.

In these experiments it is very probable that all the actions of the animals were not only performed automatically, but without the co-operation or even presence of any kind of consciousness, that is, anything like a subjective state; for the cerebral hemispheres had been removed. But in the following extraordinary case a difference of opinion has existed, and Professor Huxley in particular was led to believe from analogy with the above cases of frogs and other animals, that consciousness was not present. The case is well known and has been frequently quoted, and I should not venture to repeat it here were it not that it has an important bearing on the question under discussion, and apparently is the principal evidence upon which Professor Huxley rests his conclusions. In this case not only were all movements present which occur normally, but they were modified and adapted to changing conditions as in the normal state. If it can be shown, then, that they took place without being accompanied by consciousness, a strong case is made out for Professor Huxley's side.

The case was reported by Dr. E. Mesnet in the *Union Médicale* of July 21 and 23, 1874. The following account of it is taken from Maudsley's " Physiology of the Mind":

" A sergeant in the French army, aged 27 years, was wounded at the battle of Bazeilles by a bullet, which fractured the left parietal bone. He had power enough to thrust his bayonet into the Prussian soldier who wounded him, but almost at the same instant his right arm, and soon afterwards his right leg, became paralyzed. He lost consciousness, and only recovered it at the end of three weeks, when he found himself in the hospital at Mayence. Right hemiplegia was then complete.

" By the end of a year he had regained the use of his side, a slight feebleness thereof only being left. Some three or four months after the wound, peculiar disturbances of the brain manifested themselves, which have recurred since periodically. They usually last from fifteen to thirty hours, the sound intervals between them varying from fifteen to thirty days. These alternating phases of normal and abnormal consciousness have continued for four years.

" In his normal condition, the sergeant is intelligent, and performs satisfactorily the duties of a hospital attendant. The transition to the abnormal state is instantaneous. There is some uneasiness or heaviness about the forehead, which he compares with the pressure of an iron band, but there are no convulsions, nor is there any cry. He becomes suddenly unconscious of his surroundings and acts like an automaton. His eyes are wide open, the pupils dilated, the forehead is contracted, there is incessant movement of the eyeballs and a chewing motion of the jaws. In a place to which he is accustomed he walks about freely as usual, but if he be put in a place unknown to him, or if an obstacle is put in his way barring his passage, he stumbles gently against it, stops, feels it with his hand, and then passes on one side of it. He offers no resistance to being turned this way or that, but continues his walk in the way in which he is directed. He eats, drinks, smokes, walks, dresses and undresses himself, and goes to bed at his usual hours. He eats voraciously and without discernment, scarcely chewing his food at all, and devours all that is set before him without showing any satiety. General sensibility is lost, pins may be run into his body, or strong electric shocks sent through it, without his evincing the least pain. The hearing is completely lost; noises made close to his ears do not affect him. The senses of taste and smell are lost; he drinks indifferently water, wine, vinegar, assafœtida, and perceives neither good nor bad odors. The sense of sight is almost, but not quite lost; on some occasions he appears to be in some degree sensible to brilliant objects, but he is obliged to call the sense of touch to his aid in order to apprehend their nature, form, and position; they produce only vague visual impressions, which require interpretation into the language of touch. The sense of touch alone persists in its integrity; it seems, indeed, to be more acute than normal, and to serve almost exclusively to maintain his relations with the external world. When he comes out of the attack he has no remembrance whatever of what has happened during it, and expresses the greatest surprise when told what he has done.

"Through the tactile sense, trains of ideas may be

aroused in his mind, which he immediately carries into action. On one occasion, when walking in the garden under some trees, he dropped his cane, which was picked up and put into his hand. He felt it, passing his hand several times over the curved handle, became attentive, seemed to listen, and suddenly cried out, ' Henri,' and a little while afterwards, ' There they are, at least twenty of them ; we shall get the better of them !' He then put his hand behind his back, as if to get a cartridge, went through the movements of loading his musket, threw himself full length upon the grass, and concealing his head behind a tree, after the manner of a sharpshooter, followed, with his cane to his shoulder, all the movements of the enemy whom he seemed to see. This performance, provoked in the same way, was repeated on several occasions. It was probably the reproduction of an incident in the campaign in which he was wounded. ' I have found,' says Dr. Mesnet, ' that the same scene is reproduced when the patient is placed in the same conditions. It has thus been possible for me to direct the activity of my patient in accordance with a train of ideas which I could call up, by playing upon his tactile sensibility at a time when none of his other senses afforded me any communication with him.'

" All the actions of the sergeant, when in his abnormal state, are either repetitions of what he does every day, or they are excited by the impressions which objects make upon his tactile sense. Arriving once at the end of a corridor where there was a locked door, he passed his hands over the door, found the handle, took hold of it and tried to open the door. Failing in this, he searched for the key-hole, but there was no key there; thereupon he passed his fingers over the screws of the lock, and endeavored to turn them, with the evident purpose of removing the lock.   Just as he was about to turn away from the door, Dr. Mesnet held up before his eyes a bunch of seven or eight keys; he did not see them; they were jingled loudly close to his ears, but he took no notice of them; they were then put into his hand, when he immediately took hold of them, and tried one key after another in the key-hole without finding one that would fit.   Leaving the place, he went into one of the wards, taking on his way various articles, with which he filled his pockets, and at length came to a little table which was used for making the records of the ward.   He passed his hands over the table, but there was nothing on it; however, he touched the handle of a drawer, which he opened, taking out of it a pen, several sheets of paper, and an inkstand.   The pen had plainly suggested the idea of writing, for he sat down, dipped it in the ink, and began to write a letter, in which he recommended himself to his commanding officer for the military medal on account of his good conduct and his bravery.   There were many mistakes in the letter, but they were exactly the same mistakes in expression and orthography as he was in the habit of making when in his normal state. From the ease with which he traced the letters and followed the lines of the paper, it was evident that his sense of sight was in action, but this was placed beyond doubt by the interposition of a thick screen between his eyes and his hand; he continued to write a few words in a confused and almost illegible manner and

F                        11

then stopped, without manifesting any impatience or discontent. When the screen was withdrawn, he finnished the uncompleted line and began another. Another experiment was made: water was substituted for ink. When he found that no letters were visible, he stopped, tried the tip of his pen, rubbed it on his coat-sleeve, and then began again to write with the same results. On one occasion he had taken several sheets of paper to write upon, and while he was writing on the topmost sheet, it was withdrawn quickly. He continued to write upon the second sheet as if nothing had happened, completing his sentence without interruption, and without any other expression than a slight movement of surprise. When he had written ten words on the second sheet it was removed as rapidly as the first; he finished on the third sheet the line which he had begun on the second, continuing it from the exact point where his pen was when the sheet was removed. The same thing was repeated with the third and fourth sheets, and he finished his letter at last on the fifth sheet, which contained his signature only. He then turned his eyes toward the top of this sheet, and seemed to read from the top what he had written, a movement of the lip accompanying each word; moreover, he made several corrections on the blank page, putting here a comma, there an *e*, and at another place a *t;* and each of these corrections corresponded with the position of the words that required correction on the sheets which had been withdrawn. Dr. Mesnet concludes from these experiments that sight really existed, but that it was only roused at the instance of touch, and exercised only upon those objects with which he was in relation through touch. After he had finished his letter the sergeant got up, walked down to the garden, rolled a cigarette for himself, sought for his match-box, lighted his cigarette, and smoked it. When the lighted match fell upon the ground, he extinguished it by putting his foot upon it. When the cigarette was finished he began to prepare another, but his tobacco-pouch was taken away, and he sought in vain for it in all his pockets. It was offered to him, but he did not perceive it; it was held up before his eyes, but he took no notice of it; it was thrust under his nose, but he did not smell it; when, however, it was put into his hand he took it, completed his cigarette directly, and struck a match to light it. This match was purposely blown out, and another lighted one was offered to him, but he did not perceive it; even when it was brought so close to his eyes as to singe a few eyelashes he did not notice it, neither did he blink. When the match was applied to his cigarette, he took no notice and made no attempt to smoke. Dr. Mesnet repeated this experiment on several occasions, and always obtained the same results. The sergeant saw his own match, but saw not the match which Dr. Mesnet offered to him. There was no contraction of the pupil when the lighted match was brought close to the eye. He had once been employed as a singer at a café. In one of his abnormal states he was observed to hum some airs which seemed familiar to him, after which he went to his room, took from a shelf a comb and looking-glass, combed his hair, brushed his beard, adjusted his collar, and attended carefully to his toilet. When the glass was turned round so that he only saw the

back of it, he went on as if he still saw himself in it.
On his bed there were several numbers of a periodical
romance. These he turned rapidly over, apparently
not finding what he wanted. Dr. Mesnet took one of
these numbers, rolled it up so as to resemble a roll of
music, and put it in his hand, when he seemed satisfied,
descended the stairs, and walked across the court of the
hospital towards the gate. He was turned round, when
he started off in the new direction given to him, entering the lodge of the door-keeper, which opened into
the hall. At this moment the sun shone brightly
through a window in the lodge, and the bright light
evidently suggested the foot-lights of the stage, for he
placed himself before it, opened the roll of paper, and
sang a patriotic ballad in an excellent manner. When
he had finished this he sang a second and a third, after
which he took out his handkerchief to wipe his face.
A wine-glass containing a strong mixture of vinegar
and water was offered to him, of which he took no
notice, but when it was put in his hand he drank it off
without exhibiting any sign of an unpleasant sensation.
Dr. Mesnet propounds the question whether in this
perfect rendering of the three ballads he heard his own
voice, or whether the singing was purely as automatic
as his other actions. The attack came to an end before
they could make an experiment to test this question.
When the sergeant is in his abnormal state, it is impossible to awaken him to his normal state, whatever
efforts be made. No effect is produced either by stimulation or by strong electrical currents. On one occasion he was seized suddenly by the shoulders and
thrown violently upon the grass. He manifested no

emotion, but, after feeling the turf with his hands, raised himself again, calm and impassive.

"A remarkable feature in the case is that the sergeant becomes a veritable *kleptomaniac* during the attacks. He purloins everything that he can lay his hands on, and conceals what he takes under the quilt, the mattress, or elsewhere. This tendency to take and hide has shown itself in each attack. He is content with the most trifling articles, and if he finds nothing belonging to some one else to steal, he hides, with all the appearance of secrecy, although surrounded at the time by persons observing him, various things belonging to himself, such as his knife, water, pocket-book. His other actions during an attack are repetitions of his former habits; these acts of stealing are not so."

Professor Huxley raises the question whether this man possessed consciousness during all these performances,—*i.e.*, whether his actions were accompanied with a corresponding train of ideas; or whether the "mind is a blank," and he is in the condition of the frog deprived of his brain,—an automaton, "a mechanism worked by molecular changes in the nervous system." Professor Huxley, reasoning from the analogy which he finds in the frog, inclines to the latter supposition. That the man is an automaton there can be no doubt; but I cannot agree in thinking that ideas do not accompany his muscular movements, but, on the contrary, must believe they govern them. In the first place, as Huxley admits, there is nothing to "prove that he *is* absolutely unconscious;" and in the second place, a much stronger analogy, as Dr. Mesnet and Dr. Carpenter have pointed out, can be drawn between the performances

11*

of this man and those of somnambulists—who certainly
do possess ideas, for they remember them afterwards—
than between them and the phenomena of the brainless
frog. If the former comparison be made, the one will
be found to resemble in important particulars the other;
while if the sergeant be compared with the brainless
frog, an essential difference in the movements of the two
becomes at once apparent. In the frog deprived of his
hemispheres, the actions of its muscles are confined to
such simple movements as swimming, jumping, and
balancing itself, nearly all the motions performed by a
frog in its lifetime. Consequently the lower centres
are perfectly capable of regulating them. It is similar
with fishes which simply swim, and pigeons which fly
and dress their feathers. These actions have been so
frequently repeated that the lower ganglionic centres
carry them out automatically without the intervention
of consciousness, just as a woman knits or sews without
being conscious of what she is doing, and while her
thoughts are engaged on something else. And there is
further this peculiarity about the brainless frogs and
birds: they are absolutely machine-like in character.
The pigeon thrown into the air will continue to fly until
it strikes some obstacle or falls exhausted to the ground;
the fish will swim in the same manner, and even the
pigeon will starve though food be placed before it,
unless artificially fed like an infant. There is lacking
that quality in its actions which we call intelligence.
To be sure,—a point upon which Huxley lays considerable stress,—the frog, if a book be placed before him
and he be made to hop, will jump aside, carefully
avoiding the obstacle. But this is one of the simplest

of reflex actions, and similar to unconscious knitting, when sight directs the hands; though we do not perceive the stitches, an irritation is conveyed direct from retina to the optic thalamus and other centres for the co-ordination of sight and movement; from here the nervous current is reflected to the muscles of the limbs, and the animal springs in the required direction. This is a mechanism as simple as that observed in the well-known experiment on the amputated leg of a frog, and one which has been performed thousands of times in the frog's lifetime, and thus become impressed as it were in the nervous centres.[1]

In man there are very few movements performed unconsciously without previous education. There are some, but they are of the simplest kind, such as winking, sucking in the infant, crying, and possibly dodging the head before an expected blow, etc. Even walking is only with difficulty acquired, and it is only after it is skilfully learned that it can be performed unconsciously. It may be said that if a child were prevented from using its legs till after the age at which children usually walk, his "walking-centres" might be sufficiently developed by the natural processes of growth, as with flying in birds, to allow him to walk without education. But even so, this is not the case with such muscular actions as, for instance, are performed by

---

[1] It may be that education is not necessary for the development of the mechanism in the lower centres required for such simple movements. It has been shown, I believe, that birds, for instance, do not *learn* to fly. If they are confined so that they cannot use their wings till after the time when birds usually fly, they can fly as well as other birds who have gone through the so-called process of education.

telegraph operators. They sometimes acquire the art of telegraphing with such precision, that some are enabled to transmit a message while their thoughts are fixed upon something else;[1] that is, they do it unconsciously. A lady told me that sometimes when she finds difficulty in playing correctly on the piano a piece of music, she is enabled to accomplish it by fixing her mind upon other things. But this is only after long and hard labor at practising. In fact, it is the case with all associated movements of any degree of complexity in man, and probably also to a great extent in animals, that they first must be acquired consciously with the aid of the higher centres of ideation, before they can be performed unconsciously[2] by the lower ones. Applying this to the case of the French sergeant, we must suppose, if consciousness were not present, that he had repeatedly practised those actions he performed when he fancied the enemy in sight; and when he wrote his letter, he must have written those *same* sentences a great number of times in order to have done it *unconsciously*, and especially to have gone over it again to correct his mistakes, when only blank sheets of paper lay before him.

It was found that a certain amount of sight was present when associated with the sense of touch, and that it was necessary for guidance in writing. Now if he wrote without any ideas being present in his mind corresponding to what he wrote, that is, absolutely un-

---

[1] Carpenter's Mental Physiology.

[2] An unconscious act and an automatic act must not be confused. They are not co-extensive. An act may be automatic and unconscious, as in walking, or it may be automatic and conscious, as is all mental action.

consciously, the muscular movements of his hand must have been guided by the preceding associated movements, and by the optical excitations from the letters and words he had written. The exact part played by each it is impossible to distinguish. In the case of the telegraph operator, there is required merely an association of the optical appearance of each letter with the muscular movements required to telegraph the *same letter*, an association which has been cemented by every telegraph operator thousands of times. But with the sergeant, for the letter to have been written *unconsciously*, the optical appearance of, and muscular movement necessary for, each letter must have been firmly associated with the muscular movement needed to write each *succeeding* letter; in this way each word must have been united with each word, and phrase with phrase, and sentence with sentence. To have formed such an association, that same letter to his commanding officer must have been written hundreds of times.

In the case of the operator it is copying, in the other case it is composition. The latter is a most complicated affair, and never could have been done by the lower centres without long previous training. If ideas of what he was writing were present to his mind, there is no great difficulty in understanding the case. He wrote as a somnambulist writes, though he was not in possession of all his senses. Nor is there any great difficulty in the fact that he remembered what he wrote, when he read and corrected his letter on a blank sheet.

Further analysis would show many other facts to prove the presence of consciousness.

But there is one point which hitherto seems to have

i

escaped notice, and which, to my mind, conclusively proves that the man had consciousness, and that his actions were governed by ideas when he read his letter, and corrected and punctuated the *blank sheet of paper.* What was going on in his cerebrum during this time which could have caused him to have made the corrections? If there was not an image there, in idea, of the past composed letter, what directed the corrections? It could not have been the sight of the misspelt words, because the paper before him was blank. It may be said the movements of his lips, which accompanied the re-reading of the letter, by association, regulated the correction. But this is merely suspending the world upon the elephant, for we have then to account for the movement of the lips. But admitting it for the moment as sufficient, it is hardly possible that such muscular movements could have indicated the *misspelling* of a word unless the *idea* of the word was present to his mind. Nor would this be a satisfactory explanation for the insertion of the punctuation marks. There is no movement of the lips corresponding to a comma. How could the lips indicate there was no comma there? The only satisfactory explanation that can be offered is that the ideas which were expressed on paper actually were present to his mind; or, in other words, he possessed consciousness.

But if consciousness was present, there is nothing to show that it was not the active agent in the production of his actions. On the contrary, there is every evidence to prove that it was. All evidence, then, on the experimental side, tending to show that feeling is not the cause of our actions, falls to the ground.

# CHAPTER III.

## SELF-DETERMINATION.

THERE is one objection which is sure to be raised against the views which have been argued in the preceding pages, to the consideration of which I propose to devoté this chapter. This objection is one which has been urged, and it must be confessed with much truth, against every other theory of automatism. It arises from a fear that in some way or other a limitation will be set to the freedom of human thought. If any doctrine of automatism is inconsistent with any fact that is established directly by consciousness, it is evidence that there is a flaw somewhere in the logic. A doctrine to be sufficient must explain all the facts, whether those facts be physical or mental. If it does not do so, it is not sufficient.

I propose now to consider whether there is any fact on the side of "self-determination" with which that view of automatism which has been adopted in this work is opposed, and if there are any grounds for the fear that our mental liberty is in some way abridged by it. I may say here, in parenthesis, that any mental freedom we may have, we have; and no doctrine, as a doctrine, can abridge it, and no asseveration can give us what we have not got.

It will be my purpose to show that automatism after all is not a very terrible thing, and that when properly understood it contains nothing that is not reconcilable with popular notions regarding mental freedom. Its apparent inconsistency with that power, which each individual feels and knows he has, will be found to be only a bugbear with which to frighten the unthought-ful, and when carefully examined will be made to reveal its skeleton nature.

If by self-determination is meant the ability to direct our attention in one way more than another, to keep our thoughts occupied with one class of facts to the exclusion of others, and to make a choice when two courses of action are open to us, I know of no evidence which could be more cogent than that which we already possess pointing to the possession of such a power. I agree with Dr. Carpenter that the evidence of our own consciousness in this respect is sufficient and decisive. That I can direct my attention on any particular subject to the exclusion of other subjects, provided, of course, the circumstances under which I make the trial are not those of great excitement, is a fact of consciousness, which I can demonstrate as often as I choose to try. Each one has sufficient evidence in his own consciousness to show not only that he has the power to direct his attention, and to make a choice, when two courses of action are open to him, but that he *does* direct his thoughts, and does make such choice; *provided;* however, and this proviso is of great importance, *he has a sufficient motive to do so.* For the evidence of consciousness is equally cogent in deciding that in thus directing the course of his thoughts and making his choice it is the *preponderance of motives* which determines him. In this there is nothing that

is incompatible either with the view herein maintained
of the nature of mind, nor of the automatic character
of ideas. It is only inconsistent with that cruder form
of automatism which regards our actions as simply the
resultant of the bodily mechanism, and makes our
thoughts mere by-products, without influence upon such
actions. Such a theory of automatism could only arise
from the crudest notions of the relation between the
mind and the body.

But after having established the power of self-determination, the *agency* by which this is accomplished is
a second and further question. We say that *we* have
this power of determining our actions; but what do we
understand by this term *we?* If by it is meant, as
seems to be by Dr. Carpenter, Archbishop Manning,
and others, not only "another faculty, but, more than
this, another agent, distinct from the thinking brain,"
which directs the working of our mind and body, then
something is assumed which our conscious experience
can no longer be evoked to establish. We know by
direct consciousness that our thoughts can be determined in this or that direction, according to certain
previous desires. But I know of no consciousness
which directly informs us of the manner in which this
is done, and still less of an extra Ego over and above
our states of consciousness, which plays with our
thoughts as it would at ninepins. I can imagine a
distinct "faculty" of the mind, which is associated with
and regulates the other states of mind, but such a
faculty must be only some state of the mind itself; so
that the conditions would simply be equivalent to a
state of consciousness acting on all other states. The

12

probability of there being such faculty is another question, which I am not discussing. I know of no evidence for it, and still less for an extra independent Ego.
In my judgment, the only way in which we can ascertain the mechanism by which this self-determination
is accomplished is to study and analyze that feeling
of personality commonly called the Ego, which each
individual has. When we make use of the expressions " we," " you," etc., for the ordinary purposes of
social life, our meaning is plain enough, and it would
be mere pedantry to ask for a precise definition; we
should undoubtedly set any one down for an unmiti-
gated bore who should interrupt us with a demand for
a philosophical explanation. But in questions of this
kind involving the deeper strata of human knowledge,
it is not only not superfluous, but absolutely essential to
define exactly what is meant by every term used, when
susceptible of different interpretations. Now there are
several conceptions which may be formed of the Ego.

There is the idea of an "agent distinct from the
thinking brain," which directs our processes of thought
and bodily actions, and to which a sort of ownership
is given over all the individual portions of the body,
and the mental faculties. For any such agent as this
there is no evidence whatsoever. It is merely an abstract notion, the result of an artifice of thought, and
has no existence. Therefore, under such a conception,
the phrase " we have a self-determining power" is
philosophically empty of meaning.

Another idea of the Ego comprehends the body and
the mind united together into a whole. No particular
state of mind is thought of as differentiated from the

rest, but all possible states of mind united as an abstract notion to a body. This is much like the conception we form of another person's personality, a sort of objective Ego. We have a notion of his body, and we imagine an abstract mind, similar to our own, connected with it. We have in our thoughts no particular state of mind, as an agent, acting on the individual's body, but an abstract mind.

Another similar but less comprehensive notion of this personality is mind as a whole in distinction from the body. Both of these conceptions of the Ego are too abstract to serve the purposes of this inquiry.

That interpretation of this feeling of personality, which I conceive to be the correct one, is, that it is a compound of any given dominant state of consciousness that may be present at any moment, and other faint revived former states, and a whole stream of faint impressions more or less simultaneously coming from the periphery of the body. These last are more or less constant. I take it that consciousness at any given moment of time, where the feeling of personality is present, is always partly made up of these impressions streaming in from the periphery and constituting our consciousness of the body. On the other hand, there are times when we have absolutely no feeling of an Ego. Such times are those of deep thought or revery. In studying my own consciousness at such times (by recalling them of course afterwards to memory) I cannot recall any feeling of personality whatever. All consciousness of surroundings, of my own body, of my own Ego, disappears. I can afterwards only recall successive ideas following one another automatically without reference to the surroundings, without even any sensations from my body. Afterwards when I come to myself, as the saying goes, these successive ideas are revived faintly as memory and become joined with my now dominant state of consciousness. This latter now is also reinforced by the stream of sensations from the different portions of the body. These sensations are identical with those which have been nearly constantly experienced, and constitute my knowledge of my body. With the dominant active state of consciousness are also associated many other faint ideas or remembrances of former states. Consequently every state of consciousness where this feeling of personality is present is a compound one, consisting partly of former states revived and partly of new ones, and in many cases the new ones are but re-combinations of old ones. It is from this that the feeling of personality arises, as it seems to me. Every state of consciousness being connected with other states, some of which (sensations) are constantly or nearly constantly present, they all seem to belong to each other and to constitute a whole or Ego, and this Ego is always felt to be the same Ego, because part of its complex composition always is the same, and its elements as elements are the same.[1]

The whole mental process is undoubtedly a very complex one, with many variations, and it is almost impossible to completely analyze it. An illustration will give an idea of the principle which I conceive underlies this sense of the Ego.

---

[1] I have an impression that a somewhat similar explanation has been given by Clifford, but I have not his works by me to verify it.

I am sitting in my study of a hot day, writing. I
soon feel thirsty. This feeling grows on me till I think
of satisfying my desire. It becomes my dominant idea.
I now remember a pitcher of water standing on the
table opposite, and impressed by this idea and the effect
which I imagine will result if I pour out a glass of
water and drink it, I proceed to carry the latter into
effect. Here is a comparatively simple and yet very
complex state of affairs. Now how does the sense of
the Ego arise out of these various states of consciousness? I conceive it to be in this way.

The dominant and vivid idea "in my mind," that is,
among a complex group of ideas, is the sensation of
thirst. This sensation does not stand alone, but is
joined to other sensations from my mouth and throat,
which are the same sensations as have been constantly
present before. (For that matter, the sensation of thirst
is the same sensation often previously present in consciousness, but now re-excited, just as the molecular
disturbances underlying it are re-excited in the same
manner that they have been before.) Other sensations
from the surface of the body, the same that have been
experienced before, now reinforce the others. Besides
this, sensations from my surroundings in my study, the
same that have time and again, like the others, formed
a portion of my states of conscience, are now added to
my present complex state. Most of these sensations
are not only like but identical with previously present
sensations, which latter are simply revived. Now all
these different sensations compounded together give the
sense of personality, or the Ego, and the now dominant
sensation of thirst being added, I say, *I* am thirsty.

12*

This new sensation becomes incorporated in the group, to which other sensations, to be in turn dominant, may be added, as, again, warmth. I say, *I* am warm, the feeling of warmth being added to a group, in which the feeling of thirst now forms an element as a faintly revived state.

Such being the complex out of which the sense of personality is formed, it becomes requisite to ask which is the active agent in all this in determining action. It is undoubtedly the vivid, active state, modified more or less by the circumstances of the case. The sensation of thirst, for example, is the active agent determining me to drink some water and to the performance of the requisite actions. The method I employ to satisfy my thirst would be modified by the other elements of my complex state of consciousness, these varying with the surroundings, the time of day, and other associated ideas.

It is this complex state, then, which constitutes the Ego, and hence, as a whole, the determining agent, though some of its elements are more active than others in accomplishing the result. The most vivid and dominant element, as the feeling of thirst in the above illustration, might be regarded as the driving power, while the associated elements are the steering-gear which regulates the action.

Now in this matter of self-determination, if it be said that the Ego—being a complex state of consciousness—determines another state of consciousness that may be associated with it, with or without, as the case may be, its accompanying muscular action, the proposition is a truism which cannot be gainsaid. In this sense we certainly have self-determination, for the inducing state of consciousness is as much a part of self as the succeeding one that is determined by it.

But if, on the other hand, it be asserted that the state of consciousness called the Ego can determine any other state which is not in any way associated with it, and irrespective of all former experience by which ideas are associated, then something is maintained which is entirely contrary to all experience and indefensible. It cannot be denied that it is possible for us to act in any particular manner, provided that that idea, which is directly connected with and the precursor of the action in question, is present in consciousness, howsoever it may arise. In this sense we have self-determination, for this idea determines action. But manifestly no idea can occasion another idea, or bodily action, which is not connected with it; nor can any given state of mind or bodily action occur when the state of consciousness present is one far removed from the one in question. Furthermore, it is self-evident that no idea can arise spontaneously. Every idea is conditioned by some previous idea or stimulus, and forms a link in a chain of events.

Now if an idea which determines an action is itself determined by a preceding idea, which in turn can be traced to a still earlier one, and so on back through a chain of such ideas, until finally we arrive at a sensory stimulus of some kind, it would seem plainly evident that the final action is determined indirectly through a succession of ideas by the primary stimulus. Furthermore, it would seem that, if no disturbing element came in, that particular succession of ideas and ensuing action must result, and no other. Now this is all the

reflex theory demands, and in this there is nothing that
the most extreme defender of self-determination may
not concede.   But if the still further claim be made
that self-determination is effected by an " agent distinct
from the thinking brain," by something that is independent of our other conscious states, and is not
governed by the same laws as other states of consciousness, then something is asserted which cannot be sub-
stantiated, and which must lie outside the region of
experience, and be therefore unknowable.   For there
is nothing in our conscious experience which directly
gives us cognition of this agent, nor anything that
necessitates one hypothecating it as an explanation of
known facts.   Whether that interpretation of the sense
of personality which I have offered be the correct one,
or whether this sense arises from some other combination of mental factors, there are no more grounds for
the assumption of an autocratic Ego than there formerly was for assuming a spiritual entity for an explanation of mind.

The question may very pertinently be asked, What
manner of thing is this Ego?   Is it something akin
to that consciousness which we know is the reality
of the phenomena of matter, or is it something essentially foreign in its nature?   If the former, why, it may
be asked, is it not subject to the same laws that govern
other states of consciousness? if the latter, it must be far
beyond our ken, and the old problem becomes practically
reproduced, how can it act upon the reality of matter?

From a physiological point of view, this extreme
form of self-determination is equivalent to saying that
" we" can divert the neural current which naturally

would flow in one circuit into a different circuit, irrespective of the intensity of the molecular action, and the anatomical and physiological connections in the brain. This seems to me incomprehensible.

There is one thing which must not be overlooked, and this is, that whatever powers of self-determination we may have, every action is determined by the strongest motive. However we may act, we cannot act contrary to the strongest motive; for the moment we conclude to act in opposition to what was the strongest motive, the new motive, whatever it be, if it be only the desire to show that we have the power to do so, becomes the strongest motive, overwhelming the preceding and determining action. Whatever motive determines, action is the strongest,—else it would not so determine us,—and we are compelled to act according to it.

When we analyze our thoughts it is not always easy to make out their automatic character, so complicated is any mental action which involves any reasoning process except of the simplest kind. If we examine those mental actions which are admitted to be automatic, as when one suddenly cries out on being struck, or, to take a more elaborate example, when a school-boy recites long rules which he has learned by heart from his Latin grammar, we shall find the distinguishing characteristic to be the absence of deliberation. In fact, in many such cases the moment we deliberate we are lost. The school-boy, too, often cannot tell whether any given word is contained in a list without beginning with the first and repeating them in order.

When one idea follows another without conscious effort on our part, without that special feeling called volition, the mental action is said to be automatic; while when we have a feeling of volitional effort, or are conscious of what is called deliberation, our thoughts are declared to be automatic.

But if the reasoning which has been adduced in these pages be correct, this distinction is merely artificial; from the lowest form of mental action to the highest a gradual transition may be traced, showing that there is no difference in kind, but only one of degree. Examples of this action of the mind, when the automatic character of the ideas is plainly discernible, are more or less common in every individual, though to some they are to a large extent habitual. When we fall into day-dreams and reveries, it is very easy to recognize the automatic character of our thoughts, one follows another in natural succession, according to a previous association. On the other hand, it requires considerable introspective skill to recognize the same principle in that state of mind called deliberation, wherein the ideas, instead of following one another in progressive series without return to the original and fundamental thought, continually diverge from and return to this as a centre; thus encircling, as it were, the latter, approaching it on all sides only to leave it again by every path of ideas that may be joined by the bonds of association with it. Each "lead" of thoughts is followed, as if to see whither it goes and if it will bring us to the desired end. Just as in trying to disentangle a snarl of thread we follow each loop in turn, hoping to find the one which will unbind the whole, so in deliberation we follow each train of ideas that is associated with the central thought in the endeavor to find the one that will solve the problem.

Between these two modes of activity—Revery and Deliberation—there is every possible degree of transition, one gradually shading into the other, and it is impossible to say where one begins and the other ends.

The exalted form of the plainly discernible automatic action may often be seen in the mental activity of men of genius, in whom it is more or less habitual. Coleridge and Mozart were particularly interesting examples. The former's flow of talk has been described as only thinking aloud, and his whole life as only a waking dream. His thoughts ran on without regard to anything or anybody, heedless of interruption, while his words were only the expression of every associated and reflected idea. Mozart's genius was essentially automatic, as can be seen from the following account of his method of working :[1]

"You say you should like to know my way of composing, and what method I follow in writing works of some extent. I can really say no more on the subject than the following, for I myself know no more about it, and cannot account for it. When I am, as it were, completely myself, entirely alone, and of good cheer, say travelling in a carriage or walking after a good meal, or during the night when I cannot sleep, it is on such occasions that my ideas flow best and most abundantly. *Whence* and *how* they come I know not, nor can I force them. Those ideas that please me I retain

---

[1] See Dr. Carpenter's "Mental Physiology" for an interesting account of the automatic character of Coleridge and Mozart's minds.

in my memory, and am accustomed (as I have been told) to hum them to myself. If I continue in this way, it soon occurs to me how I may turn this or that *morceau* to account, so as to make a good dish of it,—that is to say, agreeably to the rules of counter-point, to the peculiarities of the various instruments, etc.

"All this fires my soul, and, provided I am not disturbed, my subject enlarges itself, becomes methodized and defined, and the whole, though it be long, *stands almost complete and finished in my mind,* so that I can survey it like a fine picture, or a beautiful statue, at a glance. Nor do I hear in my imagination the parts *successively*, but I hear them, as it were, all at once. What a delight this is I cannot tell! All this inventing, this pondering, takes place in a pleasing, lively dream. Still the actual hearing of the *tout ensemble* is, after all, the best. What has been thus produced I do not easily forget, and this is perhaps the best gift I have my Divine Maker to thank for.

"When I proceed to write down my ideas, I take out of the bag of my memory, if I may use that phrase, what has previously been collected into it in the way I have mentioned. For this reason the committing to paper is done easily enough, for everything is, as I have said before, already finished, and it rarely differs on paper from what it was in my imagination. At this occupation I can therefore suffer myself to be disturbed; for, whatever may be going on around me, I write and even talk, but only of fowls and geese, or of Gretie or Barbie, or some such matters. But why my productions take from my hand that particular form and style that makes them *Mozartish*, and different from

the works of other composers, is probably owing to the
same cause which renders my nose so, or so large, so
aquiline, or, in short, makes it Mozart's, and different
from that of other people. For I really do not study
or aim at any originality; I should, in fact, not be able
to describe in what mine consists, though I think it
quite natural that persons who have really an individual appearance of their own are also differently
organized from others, both externally and internally.
At least I know that I have not constituted myself
either one way or another."—*Holmes's Life of Mozart,*
p. 318.[1]

This necessary dependence of the brain upon external
stimuli for thought is well observed in social society.
It is this need which draws human beings together and
makes man a social animal. It is to these influences
that are due the charms of conversation and the pleasures to be obtained from lectures and at the theatre;
and it may be said that it is upon its emotional influence that religion depends for its power. It is through
this stimulation of the mind, the awakening into life
of the dormant cells of the brain, that we find delight
in books, in works of art, and music. It is for the
want of this that the horrors of solitude consist; we
need something to stimulate our minds. This we find
in our friendship with men, in literature, in science.
They awaken a reaction within us and give us life. By
their help we can elevate the mind to the highest stages
of development; by their complete withdrawal it is
possible to produce perfect idiocy. And just as our

---

[1] Quoted by Carpenter. Op. cit., p. 272.

muscles, from lack of use, will wither away and become useless, so will our minds under the same circumstances degenerate and become vacant; and it may be said in general that as the brain in its lowest form of development recognizes only sensation, and in its highest evolves ideas, that brain is, *cæteris paribus*, the most highly developed which is capable of responding to few thoughts of others with many of its own.

It may not be unnecessary to caution the reader not to confound this question of self-determination with that of moral responsibility. It may be thought, at first sight, that they are identical. But this is not the case. Responsibility depends upon many other factors, which are beyond my purpose to consider here.

There are, undoubtedly, many persons who, simply from conservative habits of thought, will be unable to accept the views which have been set forth in the preceding chapters. The opinions of many such are too firmly moulded by time and education to allow them to change, no matter how irrefrangible the evidence offered, and they must die in the beliefs in which they were born. Others there are who, though anxious for truth and ready to inquire into all domains of knowledge, may likewise be deterred, not so much from conservatism as by a fear that in some way the acceptance of a doctrine may lead to a limitation of mental freedom. Just as there are many persons who refuse to accept the demonstrated truths of evolution, not because of the insufficient evidence of the truth, but from a fear that some of their religious creeds may be overthrown. This sensitiveness from religious scruples

in the acceptance of scientific doctrines, which is so
marked in all departments of science, is particularly
active in inquiries into the problems offered by the
Mind. For myself, while I am able to recognize the
force of conservatism, I am unable to understand how
any right-minded person, how any one who truly seeks
after knowledge, can have any sympathy with those
who refuse to accept a doctrine, however strong may
be the evidence on which it is based, simply from
fear that when carried to its logical consequences, it
may antagonize preconceived notions. The only thing
to be dreaded in all such inquiries is that self-deception
to which the human mind is prone. I believe our aim
should be to seek the truth, and as long as we can be
assured we are on the right road, we should pursue it
wherever it may lead, and whatever may be the result.
And if it should happen that the conclusions to which
we are led are not in harmony with the popular views
of the day, though the fact may be regretted, our
results should not for that reason be discarded.

In advocating that explanation of nervous phenomena which has been maintained in the preceding
chapters, I have been actuated by the conviction that
" that theory is most deserving of credence which explains the greatest number of known facts," and I believe it has at least the merit of being free from the
mysticism with which all other doctrines are obscured.
One by one the old supernatural agents have been
weeded out of our philosophies. Formerly, whatever
in nature was beyond the comprehension of the times
was considered to have a spiritual cause. Whatever
could not be understood was accounted for by an es-

sence. Wood burned because the essence fire entered into the substance. Water was fluid because the essence aquosity permeated matter. Gradually, however, as science advanced, these essences have been gotten rid of one by one, and now but one remains. This is mind. This, in its turn, must go. It only remains to decide whether it shall be to-day or to-morrow.

# CHAPTER IV.

## WHAT IS MATERIALISM?

"BUT, as I have endeavored to explain on other occasions," says Professor Huxley, "I really have no claim to rank myself among fatalistic, materialistic, or atheistic philosophers. Not among fatalists, for I take the conception of necessity to have a logical and not a physical foundation; *not among materialists, for I am utterly incapable of conceiving the existence of matter if there is no mind in which to picture that existence;* not among atheists, for the problem of the ultimate cause of existence is one which seems to me to be hopelessly out of reach of my poor powers."[1] And "we anti-materialists," cries Mr. Fiske, in the midst of his un-called-for vituperation against materialism. Yet Huxley remarks that "thought is as much a function of matter as motion is,"[2] and Mr. Fiske's position is very much the same as that of others who call themselves materialists. What, then, is materialism?

The term materialism has no definite and determined meaning. As soon as the spiritualistic hypothesis was abandoned as untenable, and it was seen, on scientific as well as philosophical grounds, that the forces of nature were sufficient to account for the facts of consciousness as well as for that which is unconscious

---

[1] Fortnightly Review, November, 1874.
[2] Lay Sermons and Addresses, p. 338.

in nature, all sorts of interpretations sprung up and were adopted as explanations of mental facts. While the thoughtful were slow to formulate any positive opinions as to the exact conditions of the problem, others, more hasty and less philosophical, have not hesitated to advance crude and ill-digested dogmas as explanations of the mental world. But all opinions, those of the vulgar and ignorant as well as those of the learned, have been classed together, without discrimination, as modern materialism. What is still worse, the opponents of the new philosophy, without stopping to distinguish between the good and the bad, the sound and the unsound, have at times seized upon the most extreme and unsound doctrines, advanced by the hasty and irresponsible followers of the leaders in thought, and held them up to the public gaze as representative of modern materialism. Not only such unfounded doctrines as these, but their own illogical deductions from scientific truths, which they could not, or, what is to be feared is often the case, they would not understand, have been ascribed to those who do not hold them. Nor have the opponents of materialism taken the trouble to properly study and understand the true position of modern science, but falling upon some accidental inexactness of expression, have employed it as a text to assail opinions which were never maintained. It does not make the mode of attack any the less dishonest that those who have made it have stood high in public estimation. A false materialism has thus been created, the origin of which is to be found alone in the minds of those who have set themselves up as the champions of the public virtue.

The term materialism has come to be clothed with a
meaning which does not belong to it, and has been used
simply as a term of vituperation and abuse. This has
led the real exponents of the doctrine to repudiate
opinions to which false meanings have been attached,
and which have been often wilfully misunderstood.

What, then, is a materialist?

I conceive that there are two positions upon either
one of which we must stand, and between which there
is no half-way resting-place. Either all the facts of
nature with which we are conversant—both those of
the subjective world of thought and of the objective
world of things about us—are to be referred to natural
forces for their explanation, or one class of facts, the
subjective, are to be ascribed to a supernatural agent,
leaving the objective world of things for natural forces
alone. The former, under whatever interpretation it
is presented, is materialism; the latter is spiritualism.
We must accept either one or the other.

To show that matter is not what it is supposed to be
by the vulgar and ignorant, that it is something far
removed from the ordinary conception of it, is not to
remove it in any way from the field of materialism.
Nor by arbitrarily limiting the term "matter" to the
appearances of objects, and identifying those facts
which we call mind with that substratum underlying
these appearances, have we in any way avoided the
consequences of materialism. Showing that this substratum is not tables and chairs and sticks and stones
as we know them, is not to remove it from the material
world and place it in the spiritual world; to do so is
to invest spiritualism with a meaning which it does not

possess; and yet this, if I do not misunderstand him, is practically the position of Mr. Fiske. I dislike very much to ascribe opinions to any writer for fear of misrepresenting him, and therefore I speak, as Mr. Fiske himself has said, "subject to correction," and I am the more timid in this respect because the history of philosophy has shown that it is the peculiar fate of writers on abstruse subjects to be misunderstood.

As long as anything is the resultant of the forces of nature it belongs to materialism. Spiritualism, on the other hand, has always been understood to refer to something that is supernatural and is not conditioned by the laws of nature. To show, then, that matter is something else than what we have supposed it to be, is not to remove it to the realms of spiritualism, for it is still something which is conditioned by natural laws. And consequently because we have reason to believe that mind is identical with this real matter (or an "aspect" (?) of it), and is not identical with the vulgar conception of matter, we do not in any way escape from the bonds of materialism. Every one knows that thought is not stones, or sticks, or horses, or dogs, or even physical vibrations, or neural undulations; "it needs no ghost (or philosopher), my lord, to tell us this." But thought may be identical with the substratum underlying certain physical vibrations, and any doctrine which accepts this, express it in any words you please, is materialism. Any doctrine which rests content with nature, and does not introduce any supernatural element, is materialism.

By showing that there is something in nature more potent than we have ever conceived of, something which is beyond the powers of our poor senses to apprehend in its reality, materialism elevates our conception of matter and our appreciation of the powers of nature. This is a sufficient task. Unfortunately, we have all been taught to look upon matter as something inert and base. In this we have seen only with our eyes, and have not looked behind the appearances of things. Behind them nature herself lies concealed, and when she has shown herself to us in her nakedness and without disguise in the form of our thoughts, we have failed to recognize her, and mistaken her for a supernatural goblin.

We now know, thanks to science and philosophy, that matter is no longer the dead and senseless thing it is popularly supposed to be. We know that the so-called properties of matter, the shape, the color, the hardness, and other qualities of objects, do not exist outside of our own minds, but that objects as known to us are merely forms of our own consciousness. Yet, though this be true, we also know that besides these forms of our own consciousness, there is something else, which exists outside of them, and is the cause of them; that this something else consists of "activities" or "forces" of an unknown nature, and that these activities constitute the real object, the thing-in-itself. Objects, as we know them, are only sensations or modes of consciousness by which we apprehend these external activities, or, in other words, the reaction of our organism to these forces.

Matter, then, may embrace at least two conceptions (page 33), subjective matter and objective matter,—the latter being the real thing, though unknown.

Though we cannot picture to our minds the nature of these external forces, which must be forever unknown to us, Evolution teaches us that they must be allied in nature to consciousness. The elemental forces which underlie the functions of the organic world are the same as those which underlie the properties of the inorganic world. The reality of the carbon atom is the same whether it occur combined with two atoms of oxygen simply in the form of carbonic acid gas, or whether it be joined with many atoms of carbon, oxygen, hydrogen, and nitrogen in the form of a molecule of vital protoplasm. And the difference of properties and functions depends upon the greater or less complexity of the groupings of the elemental Realities. Finally, as we ascend in the scale of animal life, by more complex grouping of these elemental forces the first germs of consciousness arise, which reaches its highest development in the brain of man.[1]

The whole universe, then, instead of being inert is made up of living forces; not conscious, because consciousness does not result till a certain complexity of organization appears, but, using figurative language, it may be said to be pseudo-conscious. It is made up of the elements of consciousness. It is to these forces that are due the phenomena of the inorganic world, of life and of Mind. And when we reduce the problems of life and mind to terms of this matter, we deal with materialism. Any doctrine which recognizes these truths in this or some modified form still remains, in my

---

[1] See note to page 69. Clifford, I think, was the first to clearly recognize and formulate this principle, though glimpses of it may have been caught by others.

judgment, materialism. Matter is elevated to a higher rank, but it is still matter.

But after everything has been reduced to its lowest terms, after everything has been shown to be dependent upon the inherent forces of nature and the resultant of material conditions, have the dignity and attributes of anything that exists been in any way detracted from? Because man has been shown to be the last and highest expression in the order of development of nature, and the final resultant of those natural forces which have produced all other forms of life, have his dignity and powers as man been in any way impaired? And because mind, the *chef d'œuvre* of creation and final product of vital forces has been shown to be the outcome of the same material conditions as other vital phenomena, have its qualities been in any way impaired? Though science and philosophy may discover the causation and origin of phenomena, it cannot *by so doing* alter by a hair's breadth those phenomena themselves and make them what they are not. We may determine the elements of which any given product is composed, and ascertain the conditions by which it has arisen, but we cannot through such an analysis show that product to be anything else than what it is. The direction and energy of any force is not in any way changed by the discovery of the elementary forces of which it is the resultant.

Is the sparkle of a diamond any the less brilliant, or is the stone less valuable, because the chemist tells us, as a result of his analysis, it is nothing but carbon? The pessimist may tell us from the gloom of his half-fledged materialism that Raphael's great picture, the

Sistine Madonna, is after all nothing but paint and canvas, nothing but a conglomeration of yellow ochre, and Prussian blue, and copper green and red, spread upon some twisted and interwoven strands of flax. But after he has told us this, interesting possibly from a technical point of view if we did not know it before, he has not in any way detracted from the beauty of the picture. The picture is not yellow ochre nor Prussian blue, nor any other of these elements he has detailed, but the resultant of their combined properties, so combined that the final product is the materialized image of the great artist's conception fixed indelibly for all time. You may analyze the substance of the work till you have reduced it to its lowest chemical and physical terms, to a final conglomeration of atoms, but when you have finished there stands the picture as beautiful and as grand as ever, unaltered in a single line by your analysis and its color undimmed in a single spot. The picture is what it is, no matter what the elements may be which compose its substance; the resultant of all these forces is the picture, the finished whole.

And so it is with man. By showing that man has been slowly evolved through natural forces from the lowest forms of animal life, his powers and qualities as man have not been impaired in a single respect. There are some who fear, because the tradition has been outgrown whereby man came upon the earth as a sudden and miraculous act of creation and was deposited in a paradise where everything was prepared for his wants, that thereby his dignity as man is in some way detracted from. Just as there are some people who,

though by their superior abilities they have raised
themselves above their fellow-beings and surpassed
them in the race of life, are nevertheless ashamed of
the lowly position from which they started ; forgetting
that this very fact proves their superiority and renders
their talents more conspicuous.  It is this very disad-
vantage at the beginning which should make them
more proud of their success at the end.  And so in the
progress of evolution on this world, the fact that man
is the highest and culminating expression of nature
should render us proud of our pre-eminence and of the
exalted position we occupy.

And when we pass to those faculties which distinguish man from all other forms of creation, and make
him *facile princeps*,—his mental characteristics,—are
his intellectual or moral qualities in any way belittled
when it is discovered that these qualities are also the
products of natural forces, and are the result of the
laws of evolution?  Though we may show that the
highest flights of the intellect, the dramas of Shake-
speare, the great Cathedral of St. Peter of Michael
Angelo, and the Madonna of Raphael, are but the expression of natural forces, we do not in any way detract
from the grandeur and beauty of the work.  Nor is
the greatness of moral laws in any way impaired by
the discovery that they also owe their existence to the
slow forces of evolution, and have been dependent upon
the organic development of the brain.  Though their
germs may be found in the psychological and physiological laws governing the lowest races of mankind,
nay, further, in the lower orders of animals, the moral
laws themselves are as dominant and sublime as though

14

they were the express laws of a Creator given alone to man in his most developed state.

"Do not unto others what ye would not that they should do unto you" is no less grand in its conception because it is the resultant of material conditions. The lover will not sigh any the less " like a furnace" because you inform him his love is only the reality of molecular disturbances in his brain. We do not in any way soften the grief of the mother who mourns the loss of her first-born by telling her that her grief is the product of material factors, nor is our sympathy in any way lessened by the knowledge. She will tell you she knows nothing of all this, only that the life that is gone will never return again.

Our thoughts, our feelings, our hopes, our griefs, our pleasures, and our pains are the same and as we know them, whether their origin be found in matter or in a spirit.

But there is one respect in which materialism is far more elevating than any other doctrine. It is this. Though materialism may, in the opinion of some people, degrade man from the lofty position which, in his pride and arrogance, he had assumed for himself, and relegate him to a lowlier one at the head of the brute creation, it, on the other hand, elevates the latter to a higher station and extends the hand of sympathy to suffering, whether in man or animal. Materialism teaches us that the animals, though not so highly developed as ourselves, still differ from us only in degree, however great that degree may be. It teaches us that though their thoughts may not be as complex and extensive as our own, they still have thoughts. That·

they have emotions and sensations, pleasures and pains, like ourselves, and the lash of the whip stings as smartly as when applied to our own backs.

Materialism teaches us that, however lowly, they belong to our kith and kin, and though it may be necessary and proper that man should hold dominion over them, it should be exercised with clemency and discrimination. There can be no doubt that the belief that man is not only superior to the brute, but belongs to a supernatural order of beings, has tended to lessen our sympathy for these lower forms of creation, and blunt our sensibilities regarding them. The belief has become too general that the animal is not only a machine, but an insensible machine, and it too often happens that our sympathy remains untouched, even though the dog may lick the hand that slays it with the knife.

Nor will the morality of materialism compare unfavorably with that of any other philosophy. Materialism does not destroy morality, it merely seeks a new source for its origin. It is a fact, which no amount of analysis or scientific investigation can negative, that we have in us certain ideas and feelings, which we call principles,—moral principles. You may call these laws of thought if you please, but the class to which they belong we call moral. Under any other name they would be as real and as influential in determining our actions as that designated by the term morality. It is an interesting study to inquire into the conditions which have given rise to these laws of thought, and this science does, by investigating not only human nature as it existed in historic and, so far as is pos-

sible, in prehistoric times, and attempting to follow its
development step by step to the present time, however
imperfectly this can be done, but also by a compara-
tive study of the lower animals, and of the numerous
savage and lower races of men which inhabit the
various portions of the earth to-day.   As moral laws
are really psychological laws, this becomes a compara-
tive and historical psychology.

While the spiritualist accounts for these laws on the
principle of intuition, or, in other words, by presupposing the existence of innate ideas of right and
wrong, duty, etc., which, already developed and per-
fected, have been implanted in the mind by a Creator,
the scientific inquirer after truth, rejecting any such
lazy and unintelligent method of explaining the origin
of phenomena, seeks an explanation in natural conditions alone.   We will not here notice the miscon-
struction and personal abuse to which the latter thus
exposes himself, and that, too, simply because he pre-
fers truth, however shocking it may be to his earlier
sentiments and beliefs, to the superstitious and ignorant dogmas of passionate partisans.   I do not propose to enter here into anything of a polemical nature,
and, least of all, to say anything which may jar upon
the sentiments of any one, but to discuss the matter
before us in a straightforward and philosophical
way, without regard to preconceived opinions and
feelings.

But while the scientific investigator seeks in this
direction an explanation of these moral facts, he does
not in any way attempt to deny the existence of the
facts themselves.   On the contrary, his very inquiries

presuppose their existence, for which indeed he endeavors to account.

That the individual does possess moral principles is a psychological fact, and the belief in their validity is as cogent in regulating and governing our conduct, whether the origin of such moral beliefs shall be found in a slow psychological evolution through the force of the principle of utility, sympathy, or other equally efficient force, or in a special act of creation by which they become attributes of a spiritual essence. And it is perfectly evident that a moral principle, which has become evolved and recognized as desirable, may be impressed upon the mind by education, and so firmly implanted there through the law of association of ideas as to become a dominant factor in modifying the conduct of the individual. When once ideas have become strongly bound together by association,—and this is what moral principles are,—they exert a powerful influence over our actions and thoughts, and are not easily overcome by other feelings. In this respect they are like all other associations of ideas, the influence of which may be seen in political and religious beliefs, in our prejudices and other notions. And so strong may the influence of moral principles become from this cause that they may still continue to direct the conduct, though other processes of reasoning may logically convince us of the want of validity of the principles. Thus even those who are honestly convinced of the absence of anything obligatory in duty and other principles of ethics, still allow their conduct to be influenced by these notions, for the reason that by the time they have reached an age to think about such matters, their character has

*l*                    14*

become so formed that they can only act in opposition to it at the expense of their mental happiness. These moral principles have then become automatic, as it were. When this is the case, the same tendency to similar thought becomes transmitted to the offspring, who thus tends to inherit the same association of ideas or moral principles possessed by the parents, just as children inherit the ordinary peculiarities of character of the parents. In this respect, then, moral laws become innate or intuitive. However, it is a fact which cannot be gainsaid, that for the existence of moral principles it is requisite that the brain shall have acquired a certain degree of development. I think it will be found that moral principles become recognized as standards, even if not realized in practice, in direct proportion to the capacity of the mind to originate abstract ideas, and that in the lower races only a very low standard of ethics can prevail among those people whose minds do not rise above the conception of specific objects. Some of the tribes of Oceanica and Australia have words for particular trees, as walnut-tree or beech-tree, etc., but none for a tree in the abstract. Such people cannot possess any abstract notion of a tree or any other object or quality.

It has been said that the "lowest among the Ocean-eans and Africans (as the aboriginal Australians, the South Sea negroes, Bushmen, Central Africans, etc.) are entirely destitute of general ideas or abstract notions. Past and future concern them not. The Australian has no words to express the ideas of God, religion, righteousness, sin, etc. He knows almost no other sensation than the need of food, which he endeavors in every way to satisfy, and makes known to the traveller by grimaces. 'In them the capability of considering and inferring,' says Hale (Natives of Australia, 1846), ' appears to be very imperfectly developed. The reasons which the colonists use in order to convince or persuade them are mostly such as are employed with children and half imbeciles.' "[1]

To have any code of ethics which shall approach the standard set by civilized nations, whether these nations be composed of Christians or Buddhists, it is essential that the mind shall be sufficiently developed to conceive of abstract notions, such as ideas of right and wrong, etc., and no religion can arise till the mind is capable of entertaining the idea of causation, etc.

The animals are probably content with the simple fact of existence, and never seek to know the reason or cause for that existence, the why or the how. They accept the fact without the idea ever entering their minds of inquiring further. The lowest races of men differ from the brutes very slightly in this respect. " I frequently inquired of the negroes," says Park, " what became of the sun during the night, and whether we should see the same sun or a different one in the morning, but I found that they considered the question as very childish. The subject appeared to them as placed beyond the reach of human investigation; they had never indulged a conjecture nor formed any hypothesis about the matter."[2]

" A friend of Mr. Lang's ' tried long and patiently to make a very intelligent, docile, Australian black

---

[1] Büchner, Man in the Past, Present, and Future. Eng. Trans., p. 313.

[2] Lubbock's Origin of Civilization, Amer. ed., p. 5.

understand his existence without a body, but the black never could keep his countenance, and generally made an excuse to get away. One day the teacher watched, and found that he went to have a hearty fit of laughter at the absurdity of the idea of a man living and going about without arms, legs, or mouth to eat; for a long time he could not believe that the gentleman was serious, and when he did realize it, the more serious the teacher was, the more ludicrous the whole affair appeared to the black.'"[1] With a mind of such a character it is apparent that no religion worthy of the name could be conceived of, nor could we expect to find any moral principles of an exalted nature in force among such people. Whatever principles they may have must conduce only to the gratification of the appetites and passions.

"The aborigines of New Caledonia, akin to the Feji-Islanders, and belonging to the Papuan group, have, according to Van Rochas, no shame, go quite naked, and indulge in a number of excesses of the basest kind. They have intelligence as the beasts, but *no moral emotions*, are faithless in the highest degree, perjured, crafty, will strike any one down from behind, are cannibals, eating not merely their enemies, but even their own relatives, can only with difficulty count the lowest numbers, use strong abortives, and bury the aged alive. If a chief is hungry, he straightway knocks down one of his subjects."[2]

"The Australians," says a lady who emigrated to Australia, "live quite naked in huts of bark, in which

[1] Lubbock's Origin of Civilization, Amer. ed., p. 245.
[2] Büchner, op. cit., p. 315.

they sleep with their dogs. They eat anything,—insects, serpents, worms, roots, berries, etc.,—have no fixed dwelling-place, and are quite incapable of civilization. The missionaries have long given up every attempt to civilize them, for if one baptize them it has no more effect than the baptism of a dog or a horse; they understand nothing of the signification of the act. Marriages are very loose, infanticide is universal, the aged are put to death. They live only in the present, and think neither of the past nor the future. They cannot be taught any principles. They are dead to all morality. They know no sentiment, no spiritual life, no love, no gratitude, but only unbridled passion, and the sense of their nothingness against the white races."[1]

But there is one mistake easy to fall into in considering the state of morality of communities, and this is to assume, because of the absence in the lower races of the moral laws which prevail among highly civilized nations, that therefore the former are totally lacking in morality. On the contrary, they often have laws which though to us seemingly absurd and without reason, and not existing among civilized peoples, yet belong to the moral class, and prohibit, under the most stringent punishment, practices which are perfectly justifiable under our systems of government and codes of ethics. For example, among those nations which practice exogomy, that is, marriage only with individuals of a foreign tribe, marriage within the tribe is regarded as incest, and is punishable with death. This

---

[1] Büchner, op. cit., p. 314.

is the case among the Kurnai[1] in Australia. Such
people would regard our practice of marrying within
our own caste or nationality as highly immoral and in-
cestuous. One rather amusing custom among these
people and, strangely enough, quite commonly diffused
among similar tribes throughout the globe, is that of
forbidding all social intercourse between mother-in-law
and son-in-law.[2] After marriage the son-in-law is not
allowed even to speak to his mother-in-law.

Numerous other customs of a more important character, and which exert considerable influence upon the
character of the race, might be mentioned as prevalent
among various races low in the scale of development.

Mr. Galbraith, who lived for many years, as Indian
agent, among the Sioux (North America), thus describes
them: they are " bigoted, barbarous, and exceedingly
superstitious. They regard most of the vices as virtues. Theft, arson, rape, and murder are among them
regarded as the means of distinction; and the young

---

[1] " The Kamilaroi and Kurnai," by Lorimer Howitt and A. W.
Fison.

[2] " A Brabotung, who is a member of the Church of England,
was one day talking to me. His wife's mother was passing at
some little distance, and I called to her. Suffering at the time
from cold, I could not make her hear, and said to the Brabotung,
' Call Mary, I want to speak to her.' He took no notice whatever, but looked vacantly on the ground. I spoke to him again
sharply, but still without his responding. I then said, ' What do
you mean by taking no notice of me?' He thereupon called out
to his wife's brother, who was at a little distance, ' Tell Mary
Mr. Howitt wants her.' And turning to me, continued, reproach-
fully, ' You know very well I *could not* do that; you know
I cannot speak to that old woman.' "—*Kamilaroi and Kurnai,*
p. 203.

Indian from childhood is taught to regard killing as
the highest of virtues. In their dances, and at their
feasts, the warriors recite their deeds of theft, pillage,
and slaughter as precious things; and the highest, indeed, the only ambition of a young brave is to secure
'the feather,' which is but a record of his having
murdered or participated in the murder of some human
being,—whether man, woman, or child, it is immaterial;
and after he has secured his first 'feather,' appetite is
whetted to increase the number in his cap, as an Indian
brave is estimated by the number of his feathers."[1]

These Indians it is evident had moral laws, though
they were of a very opposite standard from our own.
It was probably a moral law which induced the Spar-
tans as well as savages to destroy the sickly children.

The extent to which some of the lower races will
sacrifice their own feelings to their sense of duty, however distorted the latter may appear to us, is not often
surpassed by more civilized people.

"The Feejeeans believe that 'as they die such will
be their condition in another world; hence their desire
to escape extreme infirmity.' The way to Mbulu, as
already mentioned, is long and difficult; many always
perish, and no diseased or infirm person could possibly
succeed in surmounting all the dangers of the road.
Hence as soon as a man feels the approach of old age,
he notifies to his children that it is time for him to die.
If he neglects to do so, the children after a while take
the matter into their own hands. A family consulta-
tion is held, a day appointed, and the grave dug. The

---

[1] Lubbock's Origin of Civilization.

aged person has his choice of being strangled or buried alive. Mr. Hunt gives the following striking description of such a ceremony once witnessed by him. A young man came to him and invited him to attend his mother's funeral, which was just going to take place. Mr. Hunt accepted the invitation and joined the procession, but surprised to see no corpse, he made inquiries, when the young man ' pointed out his mother, who was walking along with them as gay and lively as any of those present, and apparently as much pleased. Mr. Hunt expressed his surprise to the young man, and asked him how he could deceive him so much by saying his mother was dead, when she was alive and well. He said, in reply, that they had made her death-feast, and were now going to bury her; that she was old, that his brother and himself had thought she had lived long enough, and it was time to bury her, to which she had willingly consented, and they were about it now. He had come to Mr. Hunt to ask his prayers, as they did those of the priest.

" ' He added that it was from love for his mother that he had done so; that in consequence of the same love, they were now going to bury her, and that none but themselves could or ought to do such a sacred office! Mr. Hunt did all in his power to prevent so diabolical an act; but the only reply he received was that she was their mother, and they were her children, and they ought to put her to death. On reaching the grave, the mother sat down, when they all, including children, grandchildren, relations, and friends, took an affectionate leave of her; a rope made of twisted tapa was then passed twice around her neck by her sons, who took hold of it and strangled her; after which she was put in her grave, with the usual ceremonies.

"So general was this custom that in one town containing several hundred inhabitants Captain Wilkes did not see one man over forty years of age, all the old people having been buried."[1]

On the other hand, as Lubbock has pointed out, a state of society where vice and crime are absent do not necessarily indicate a high *moral* standard. It may simply be due to negative virtue, to an absence of any inducement to commit crime, or to a mind so imperfectly developed as to be devoid of appetites or a desire to gratify them. Such persons can no more be praised for virtue than can the domestic cow be deserving of reward for refraining from murder or other human vices.

For the conception of a code of morality similar to that embraced by Christianity and Buddhism, there is required a brain of high organization. Though the converse is not true, that a highly organized brain implies a high standard of morality, it only signifies the possibility of such a standard. There are large numbers of other conditions, those embraced under the social and political forces which determine the nature of the moral code in force among any people at any particular epoch. These conditions are beyond our purpose to consider here, but I would call attention to the fact that a distinction must be drawn between the theoretical and practical morality of a community, between the moral principles exemplified in the life of

---

[1] Lubbock's Origin of Civilization, p. 248.

the masses of the people and that standard advocated
and practised only by the moral specialists.   Just as
at a time when the pagan Greeks were worshipping
their false gods, the philosopher wise above his time,
six hundred centuries before the birth of Christ, smiled
at the simplicity and credulity of his fellows while he
sang :

" There is one God supreme over all gods, diviner than mortals,
   Whose form is not like unto man's, and as unlike his nature ;
" But vain mortals imagine that gods like themselves are be-
      gotten,
   With human sensations and voice and corporeal members ;
" So, if oxen or lions had hands that could work in man's
      fashion,
   And trace out with chisel or brush their conception of god-
      head,
   Then would horses depict gods like horses, and oxen like oxen,
   Each kind the divine with its own form and nature endow-
      ing." [1]

In estimating the moral condition of a people, as
Lecky has well remarked, it is necessary to consider
both the moral code advocated as a standard and the
actual habits of the people themselves.[2]

---

[1] Xenophanes of Colophon.

[2] " In estimating, however, the moral condition of an age, it
is not sufficient to examine the ideal of moralists.   It is necessary, also, to inquire how far that ideal has been realized among
the people.   The corruption of a nation is often reflected in the
indulgent and selfish ethics of its teachers ; but it sometimes
produces a reaction, and impels the moralist to an asceticism
which is the extreme opposite of the prevailing spirit of society.
The means which moral teachers possess of acting upon their
fellows vary greatly in their nature and efficacy, and the age of
the highest moral teaching is often not that of the highest gen-

For a high standard of morality not only is it essential that the brain should be highly developed and capable of forming abstract conceptions, which shall be so firmly implanted in it, as it were, as to automatically govern our thoughts and actions, but the acquisition of extended experience and knowledge is necessary for the development of these moral conceptions. When this latter is lacking we find either the moral standard is low, or, if high, is only in practice of limited application. Thus the Indian, who regards the murder of one of his own tribe as a moral crime, considers the killing of an individual of a foreign tribe as the highest virtue. And even among nations boasting of Christian civilization, we find different standards of ethics in force within the nation from that which it practises between itself and foreign nations. National and international ethics are two different things. When our knowledge becomes so far extended that each nation shall perceive that the results of a high degree of morality will be as beneficial to a nation in its relations to another as in the relations between individuals, a much higher international moral code will be established than exists to-day, and as the principles become ingrained in the mind, they will tend by inheritance and education to become automatic and dominant in regulating international conduct.

After those modes of thought called moral principles have become established and automatic, it makes no

eral level of practice. . . . In addition, therefore, to the type and standard of morals inculcated by the teachers, an historian must investigate the realized morals of the people."—*Lecky's History of European Morals. Preface.*

difference by what process they have become evolved. Whatever it may be, their influence in dominating the conduct is the same. We refrain from doing any act because we think it is wrong, and we do something else because we think it is right, and we judge it is right or wrong according as it is or is not in harmony with certain fixed principles which have been formulated as standards.

But while this is the case, the different schools of philosophy markedly differ in the incentives which each offers to induce an adherence to moral principles.

In the theological school a system of rewards and punishments plays a very important part at least, and in the past has played a greater part. People have been taught to act honestly and uprightly in order that they may hereafter be rewarded, and warned against immorality by the fear of future punishment. We are urged to a certain course of action for our own good and for our own benefit. Compare such a code with that offered by materialism and see if the latter loses by the comparison. Instead of being reminded of reward and punishment, we are told to act uprightly for the common benefit of humanity and of the human race, not for the sake of benefiting ourselves alone. The individual is educated to regard the good of the many as that for which the individual should strive, and his reward and punishment is to be found in the happiness or unhappiness of his fellow-beings.

An Italian Jesuit priest, who made it his duty to attend those dying in one of our hospitals and help their souls onwards as they started on their final journey, once fell into argument with me on the subject of religion. Becoming finally heated with the argument, he exclaimed, with more candor than caution, "I do not care for the broken arms and the broken legs; the hospital might burn up, I would not care. *It is a little corner for myself in the beautiful land I wish to make.*" I suppose that he regarded each soul saved as scoring one for himself.

Though no one would impute such selfish motives to the majority of mankind, still it is hard to deny that they enter into theological morality.

Though this system may be justified by the fact that the world is not yet prepared for a higher code, such as that offered by materialism, the system is not thereby elevated. It is a fact, and a melancholy one, that human nature is weak, and in its present state of development requires to be stimulated by the promise of reward, and to be checked by the threat of punishment; and so-called moral philosophers would, if they were really philosophers, recognize this fact with its necessary consequences, and cease to rail at the existing order of things, and refrain from thrusting their own systems of philosophy, however elevating theoretically, upon a world unprepared for them.

Theological ethics is that best suited for the control of man as he now exists. Whether mankind will in the future attain to a degree of development which will enable the individual to perform a duty for duty's sake, without hope of reward or fear of punishment, is a question which belongs to the domain of speculation.

At present, however humiliating may be the thought, man, like the brute, can only be tamed and morally educated by the alternate use of sweetmeats and the lash.

15*

www.ingramcontent.com/pod-product-compliance
Lightning Source LLC
Chambersburg PA
CBHW031112020726
47495CB00007B/2163